WAKE ME UP BEFORE YOU GO-GO
A JUSTICE SECURITY NOVEL

By

T. M. Bilderback

Copyright 2013 by T. M. Bilderback

For Christi

My support,
My inspiration
My everything.

Chapter 1

The alarm clock began its shrill screaming at five PM. Resisting the almost overpowering urge to pick the damn thing up and hurl it across the room, Brandon King reached over and gently turned it off. Before he could succumb to the enticements of just a *few* minutes more sleep, he turned the covers back and dragged himself out of bed.

New assignment tonight. Gotta look sharp. Gotta BE sharp! Teaming with Patty again.

Brandon glanced over at Chris's side of the bed. *I like this assignment, but it sure messes up our time together.*

He padded to the bathroom to shave and shower. As Brandon shaved, he thought about his assignment for the last week.

Brandon King was a "grunt" – a uniformed security officer with Justice Security. Brandon took his job *very* seriously. He had been noticed by Joey Justice, the leader of the company, and his partner, Percival "King Louie" Washington. Louie had invited Brandon to talk with him about going plainclothes. Brandon had initially been excited, but, upon reflection, he had turned the offer down. As he had told Louie, he felt that he needed a bit more "seasoning" on the front lines, but he hoped that the offer would come again.

"Brandon," Louie had told him, "The offer is a standing one. When you think you're ready, come see me. De job will be yours, man."

It was nice to know that the big bosses thought so much of him.

Brandon had a Bachelor's degree in Criminal Justice. He was taking online classes, working toward his Master's degree. Once he had that, he would consider whether he wanted to pursue a doctorate.

He was twenty-one years old.

Brandon turned on the shower, and stepped into the refreshing spray. He stood there, letting the warm water wake him up as it hit him, thinking.

When he had told Patty Ferguson, his best friend and partner, about the offer, she said, "I knew about it. Miss Wilhite offered me the promotion, too."

"Did you take it?" asked Brandon.

Patty had smiled, and punched him on the arm. "What do *you* think?"

Patty was doing the same educational things that Brandon was doing, but she had a spark of ambition that occasionally overtook her good judgement. But, not in this case – she had remained a grunt.

"When we go plainclothes, we go together," she said. "That's what best friends *do!*"

Brandon stepped out of the shower, toweled off, then prepared to shave. As he was lathering his face, he reflected on his current assignment.

A new club in town, called simply, "*Wham*", had decided they needed more security than just a couple of bouncers, and had hired Justice Security. As a result, *Wham* had four grunts and two plainclothes people during open hours. The club manager said that he had received several threats, and that the club's owner had instructed him to hire extra security, and had specified Justice Security.

Brandon had been assigned to the club for the past three nights. It had been simple enough, but, for some reason, Tony Armstrong, Justice Security's head grunt, had teamed Brandon with Jim Crowe, and they had been covering the entrance together. Crowe's condescending and rather bossy manner to the patrons had driven Brandon crazy, and left him wondering why one of the patrons had not punched Crowe in the mouth. Finally, he had enough, and last night, Brandon called Tony, and asked to be reassigned...or to have Crowe reassigned.

"Yeah, kid, I know what you're sayin'," Tony had said. "Your plainclothes have already complained. You held out longer than most people have. Let's see..." Brandon could hear paper rustling. "Okay, your friend, Patty, is free starting tomorrow night. I'll put her with you, and I want you two prowling inside the club. I can't call Crowe off yet – I don't have anybody to replace him...but I can team somebody else with him at the door. How's that?"

"Thank you, Tony," Brandon had replied. "I was afraid that I'd punch him myself."

Tony had laughed. "I know, kid, I know!"

"Hey, Tony?"

"Yeah, Brandon?"

"Who's gonna be the plainclothes?"

Brandon had heard Tony shuffling papers again. "Looks like...hey, you and Patty hit the jackpot. You got the big man himself, and his lady friend."

Joey Justice and Misty Wilhite. While he was teamed with Patty.

Gotta look sharp. Gotta BE sharp! he thought again, as he rinsed shaving cream remnants off of his face.

THE ETERNAL QUANDARY with this job isn't whether I should rough somebody up, or shoot them, or report them for a criminal act. The eternal quandary is this: Since I'm working at Wham *tonight, should I be minimal with the makeup, or should I give it the full Monty...I mean, the full Patty?*

Patty Ferguson looked at her reflection in the bathroom mirror. Her blond hair framed a face with very attractive, delicate features. Her deep blue eyes did not betray her emotions or her thoughts. The light freckles across the bridge of her nose and the top part of her cheeks suggested an outdoorsy private life.

Not so. Patty *hated* the outdoors. Every time she had ever gone camping or hiking, something bad had happened to change her mind about how "great" the outdoors were. Her parents had been big outdoorsy people, and had always taken her and her brother camping for a week every single summer. One year, she had been fishing at the upstate lake they always went to, when her line went taught, and she began reeling it in, fighting with whatever had taken the bait. As she finally got the line reeled in close enough for her father to use the net, they discovered that she had hooked a huge snapping turtle, with a shell that was a good fifteen inches across. Her father brought the turtle into the boat to attempt to draw out the hook from the poor turtle's jaw, but this proved impossible. The turtle's temperament, pain, and fear made it very aggressive. It had almost taken various fingers and toes from Patty and her family before her father cut the line and tossed the turtle over the side. He left the hook in place, giving the turtle a nice piercing to impress its turtle friends. Another time, while hiking on one of the summer outings, she had left the trail to urinate. She didn't recognize the leaves she squatted in as poison oak, and spent a couple of weeks itching in all of her most embarrassing spots.

So, no...Patty was *not* an outdoorsy type, unless it involved sidewalks, pavement, and the city.

Patty *was,* however, a grunt...with Justice Security, no less! She was very proud of that fact, and that she had been able to stay close to her best friend from high school through her working life a few years later. So far, anyway.

Sometimes, Patty wished she had accepted the promotion to plainclothes. But, if she had, she knew that she wouldn't have the opportunity to work with Brandon very often.

She had told Misty Wilhite, "No, I think I should stay a grunt for now. Brandon and I can do more good this way. At least, for a while."

Misty had smiled. "I understand, Patty. Let me know when you're ready. The job will be there."

But...on nights like this, working security for the hottest new club in town...if she were plainclothes...

Screw it! Uniform or not, it's the full makeup job!

Patty began making herself up.

"MISTY! ARE YOU GOING to be in there all *night?*" said Joey Justice through the bathroom door.

"I told you, I'm putting on my face," replied Misty.

"Why? Did it fall off?"

"Spoken like a man that wants to spend the night on the sofa..."

"Just kidding, sweetheart."

"Uh-huh..."

"We've got some time before we have to leave...I'd like to get in a quick nap. Will you wake me up in about an hour, before we go?"

"Yes, Joey, I'll wake you up before I go. After all, I'm not planning on going solo to this thing."

"Thanks, honey. I love you!"

TONY ARMSTRONG WAS giving Mark Haase, the night desk guy, a quick turnover before turning over the front desk to him.

"And don't forget, Mark, I'm pulling a double tonight," Tony said to Mark. "I'm working the uniform shift tonight at *Wham*. I've had so many complaints about Jim Crowe, that I gotta observe him firsthand."

"Have the complaints been that bad?" asked Mark.

"More than I want to talk about. More than we should have for a grunt."

"What's the panic word?"

"Jitterbug. In the unlikely event that you hear one of us say it tonight, send everybody. We'll be in deep do-do."

"At least you'll have the kids with you tonight. And the big bosses. That might help with Crowe."

Tony chuckled. "I sure hope Crowe doesn't mess up tonight with Joey there. He'll find himself bounced outta there on his ass...and the boss'll be doing the bouncing!"

"SIR, I THINK IT WILL be tonight."

"I certainly hope it is so. I am not a man known for my patience."

Chapter 2

Promptly at six-thirty, Patty opened her front door. Brandon stood straight, with his hands tucked behind his back. His uniform looked freshly pressed, and his shoes looked freshly polished. The two-toned brown uniform of Justice Security was highlighted by Brandon's coffee-with-cream complexion. His sidearm shined, and his badge sparkled.

Patty, of course, looked just as shiny and impressive.

"Ready?" asked Brandon.

"All set," replied Patty. "You look *sharp,* dude!"

Brandon displayed a hint of a smile. "So do you, sweet lady."

"Then let's go knock the socks off of these clubbers!"

"...JOEY...JOEY...WAKE up, sweet man..."

Joey woke with a start. He looked up at Misty, and actually gasped.

"My God," he said with awe. "You look beautiful, Misty!"

She smiled demurely. "Do you really think so?"

Joey closed his mouth with a snap. "Oh, yeah."

Misty was wearing a form-fitting maroon dress. It came to mid-thigh, and left little to the imagination...without revealing anything. Her hair hung to her shoulders, with a hint of curl at the ends. Her makeup was very understated, and you could almost believe that she wasn't wearing any. She wore open-toed, one-half-inch heels, and her skin tone made stockings unnecessary. A beautiful woman anytime, she resembled a magazine model more than a security specialist.

"I am the luckiest man in the world," said Joey. "Why does a woman like you want to marry a man like me?"

Misty put her arms around his neck. "Because you make me feel special, Joey Justice."

She kissed him. Several times.

A FEW MINUTES LATER, as they passed the front desk, Mark Haase greeted them.

"Mark, can you refresh our memories with tonight's panic word? Joey seems to think it's 'oh, baby'..." said Misty with a giggle.

Mark laughed. "It's 'jitterbug', Misty."

"Jitterbug," said Joey, mostly to himself. "Got it."

"Do you know who's scheduled with us tonight, Mark?" asked Misty.

"Sure," said Mark, consulting his computer screen. "Brandon, Patty, Crowe, and Tony."

"Tony?" asked Joey.

"He wants to observe Crowe. He's had a lot of complaints."

Joey nodded. "Let's hope for a quiet night, and a saved job for Crowe."

"Amen. Good luck, you two...and be careful. I'll be monitoring here."

Misty smiled. "Thanks, Mark."

NO ONE COULD SAY WHO was the architect of *Wham*. It *was* a new club, just finished a couple of months earlier, and was one of the more unusual buildings in the city. It stood two stories tall, with minimal windows on the second floor only, none on the first floor, and was an art deco fanatic's nightmare. The steel-reinforced front doors were over eight feet tall, and each half was four feet wide. Weatherproof carpet lined the sidewalk leading to the front stairs, and on the stairs themselves. A red velvet chain was draped across the sidewalk, and two strong, bulky men – club employees, and one armed with a clipboard – guarded the sidewalk with enthusiasm. Only certain people were allowed to enter the club, and no pattern or criteria for entry could be detected by the customers. There *were* guidelines for entry, but were designed to be low key, and not discernable.

Just inside the entrance, there was a foyer that contained a coat-and-hat-check station, attended by two lovely ladies in skimpy costumes. Past the check station, a set of five stairs led up, then seven stairs on the opposite side led down to the club proper. Just before customers climbed the stairs, they encountered two Justice Security grunts. They were posted there, checking IDs and generally making sure that the customers weren't dangerous. This is the spot that Brandon had been posted to the past few nights, partnered with Jim Crowe.

On the other side of the stairs, on the floor of the club, many tables, booths, and private rooms were scattered around the edges of the main floor of the club, which was three feet below the edges, and was referred to as "the pit". Some of the private rooms were *very* private, with enough soundproofing to allow the customer to close out the noise of the music and the people. Business of an illegal kind was often conducted in these private rooms...but, Justice Security had only been hired to keep the peace, not bust people for private business conducted behind closed doors. However, one standing rule handed down to each grunt was that injury to a person or a group of people would not be tolerated, and all personnel were expected to intervene, either alone or with assistance.

Grunts were also expected provide backup the two burly gatekeepers outside, but only when called. The manager, Ray Pruett, was very explicit with these instructions.

"If someone should ask for your help, you're expected to provide it. Otherwise, your post is inside...got it?" Pruett had instructed.

Grunts were also expected to arrive before anyone in plainclothes, but the plainclothes people arrived at different times. No one was to figure out that two plainclothes security personnel circulated among them, and by staggering hours and rotating personnel, no one should guess that Justice Security was anywhere except in uniform.

Security cameras, *not* installed or operated by Justice Security, were in place throughout the club. Some could be seen...but some blended very well into the décor.

The blueprints were on file downtown in the city's Hall of Records office. They were quite accurate as of the filing. The finished building, however...that was something else entirely. Many changes costing hundreds of thousands of dollars had been made. Thanks to certain bribes, threats, and the use of blackmail, these changes were not recorded anywhere, and were not known to anyone, except the owner, manager, and certain contractors that built the changes into the building.

Brandon King and Patty Ferguson, unaware of contractors or building changes, arrived at the club at six-fifty PM in Brandon's Porsche Boxster, ten full minutes before the doors opened to admit the public. Brandon's Boxster was an older model, but it was still a Porsche, and he was quite proud of it...he had bought it himself, without family money to back him up. Showers were in the forecast for later in the evening, so Brandon pressed the button that closed the convertible top, then he and Patty got out of the car and walked to the employees' entrance.

"So Chris isn't jealous of me any more?" asked Patty.

Brandon shook his head. "Nah. Chris finally realized that 'friend' does not equal 'girlfriend'" He laughed. "Although it seems that I spend more time with you than I spend with Chris!"

Patty linked her arm into his. "And that's why we're best friends."

Brandon stopped walking, and turned Patty to him. He took her hand and put it in the center of his chest.

"Feel that?" he asked.

Patty could feel the faint beat of his heart. "What? Your heartbeat?"

Brandon nodded. "You put the beat into my heart, Patty. You're my touchstone. My rock. There are families that are never as close as you are to me. You *are* my best friend, and you always will be."

Patty's eyes started tearing. She looked down before Brandon could see how deeply he had touched her. She regained her composure and looked into his eyes.

"Come on, you," she said to him. "Let's go to work."

They joined a group of employees and went inside the club.

JOEY AND MISTY WERE driving to the club. Traffic grew a bit heavier as they got closer. As Joey shifted the car down into second, he spoke.

"Misty?"

"Hmmm?"

"When are we going to announce our engagement?"

Misty was silent for a moment as she watched other traffic outside the car.

"When I'm convinced that you really mean it," she replied, quietly.

Joey looked at her. The hurt he was feeling was plainly evident on his face.

"Do you mean that?" he asked.

"Oh, Joey, I know you love me. That's not the question. The question is in two parts: One, why did you wait so long? And, two, why haven't you shouted it from the rooftops that I said yes?"

Joey flipped on the turn signal and pulled over to the side of the street. He turned on the emergency flashers and turned to face her.

"I waited so long because *you* wanted to wait. I haven't shouted it from the rooftops because I thought we'd shout it together."

Misty was looking at her lap. She nodded.

"Say I believe that," she said quietly. "When do we shout it together?" She looked up at his eyes. "When does everyone find out that you finally think that I'm good enough to marry?"

Joey returned her look steadily, and took Misty's hand. "I'm ready any time, sweet woman. I will be by your side, then...and always."

Misty saw the truth in Joey's eyes, and smiled. They leaned closer, and kissed...and traffic passed their parked car unheeding, and unheeded. After a while, the windows fogged, and time was forgotten.

"STEVE, FOR CHRIST'S sake, can't you keep up?" said Miriam Apple, Channel 7 spot news reporter. "I mean, it's a friggin' *camera!* How can it be keeping you from staying with me?"

Steve, the faithful cameraman, stopped walking. Miriam walked a few more steps until she realized that he was no longer walking with her. She stopped and turned.

Steve had stopped, and was aiming the camera at her expectantly.

"What are you...?" she started, as she looked around.

Miriam was about fifteen paces away from the front of *Wham,* the hot new nightclub. Her producer, a gray-haired, overweight man named Tim Wilson, had sent her there to do a fluff story. A *fluff* story, for Christ's sake! An Emmy-winning, Pulitzer-nominated news reporter, reduced to a *fluff* story! Her producer was a grudge-carrying *asshole!*

Of course, it never occurred to her that she didn't get assigned to the fluff story until *after* she had told him that he was a grudge-carrying asshole.

And now, here was Steve, in perfect position for her to do her opening shot, establishing that the story was about *Wham*.

"Oh," she said. She prepared to do her opening, cursing Steve the entire time.

Steve kept quiet, and waited patiently.

Miriam adjusted her wireless microphone, and nodded to Steve. "Okay, you gutless wonder...let's do this and get it over with!" She smiled her award-winning smile and began to speak.

"*Hi!* I'm Miriam Apple, reporting to you tonight from the hottest nightclub in town, *Wham!*" She waved behind herself, effortlessly pointing in the correct position to 'display' the red neon cursive lettering that spelled out the name of the club. "I'm going to take you behind the scenes, and show you what makes this club so popular!" She continued to smile for a few seconds, then said, "Okay, cut it. How was it?"

Steve nodded.

"Of course it was great...it was *me!* Come on – let's go find the manager of this place." She started toward the entrance. "I just hope that stupid, selfish, asshole Wilson remembered to call ahead and grease the skids for me."

Several people were already in line for the doors. A tall, muscular man showed them a palm at the velvet rope. "Sorry, folks, we're not open yet. Come back in ten minutes."

Miriam sighed, disgusted. "I'm Miriam Apple from Channel 7 News, and this is Steve, my cameraman. Your manager should be expecting us."

The man smiled and said, "Of course, Ms. Apple. I didn't recognize you. You're much more attractive in person." He held the door open for them.

Miriam gave the man a sardonic smile. "Nice save, buster," she told him as she and Steve entered the club.

PERCIVAL "KING LOUIE" Washington was enjoying a quiet, moderately expensive dinner at an exclusive restaurant in the city. Sharing dinner with him was a tall, very attractive lady named Donna Yarbrough. Donna was a *very* highly paid fashion model.

Louie had been christened with his nickname years earlier, in college, by his friend Misty Wilhite, because of an unfortunate facial resemblance to the King Louie character in *The Jungle Book*. If Louie had had a big nose, Misty would have christened him "Baloo". His college friends, the three other founding members of Justice Security, made sure that the name stuck. Louie didn't really mind. The nickname was much better than being called "Percy".

Louie was explaining all of this to his dinner date. The lady was polite enough to chuckle at the correct places. Louie had begun speaking with what he called his "Eee-bonic crapspeak".

"So, here ah is, at college, runnin' 'round with this nickname give to me by a little nuthin' of a girl. All de racists thought it was a dee-rogatory name, and so did a lot of bruthas! But, it was the farthest thang from the truth. It was all because ah looked lak somebody in Misty's favorite movie." Louie took a bite of his salad, chewed for a moment, then said, "And I've worn that name proud ever since."

Donna put down her fork and said, "Louie, may I ask you something?"

Louie put down his own fork, and replied, "Sho' can, ma'am."

She smiled at his small joke. "I've known you for about a month now..."

"A month and three days," finished Louie. "But who's counting, right?"

Donna smiled at Louie again. "A month and three days, then. In that time, I've seen several sides of you. I've seen the athlete. I've seen the man of depth and feeling. I've seen the man of research and education, and I've seen the man of violence...but only when it's necessary, or when it's warranted."

"And your point? Or your question?"

"Out of all the men I've seen you become, the one I dislike is this one-dimensional, ebonics-spewing, black idiot. *Why* do you do it, Louie?"

Louie stared at her with his mouth slightly open. After a moment, he threw his head back and started laughing. He laughed so hard that other patrons turned to stare at him, and he had tears in the corners of his eyes.

"Oh, baby, thank you," he said after he had calmed down a little.

The lady had been laughing as well...Louie's laugh was a bit contagious. "Why are you thanking me, sweetie?" she asked.

Louie took her hand. "*You* are the first person that's been brave enough to ever ask!" he responded. "The answer is simple, especially for someone that grew up in Alabama. There were still parts of that godforsaken state that looked at black people as vermin...or worse. You learned quickly to speak with that 'eee-bonic crapspeak' to keep from drawing attention to yourself when you spoke to 'white folk'. Sure, it's demeaning, and it's one-dimensional...but, for *there*, and *then*, it was survival. Now? Sometimes, when I'm comfortable and not paying attention to how I speak, I slip back into it...and I don't know it." He leaned closer to her, and said, "My mama, Betty, has been after me for *years* to stop it. Now you. I will make a concerted effort to drop dat habit from mah speechifyin'. How dat, baby?"

Donna smacked Louie's hand, and smiled. "Thank you, sir."

"Glad to be of service, Donna. Now, how about dessert?" replied Louie, gesturing for the waiter.

AT THE JUSTICE SECURITY building, in one of the partner apartments on the sixth floor, founding partner Dexter Beck was at home, meditating. Or trying to. He found it was very difficult to meditate when his new bride and newest business partner, Megan Fisk Beck, was grinding her breasts against the side of his head.

"Dexxxxxterrrrr," she said whiningly. "Let's go playyyy!"

"Please, Megan," Dexter replied. "Let me meditate for a few minutes. Then we'll play, okay?"

Megan stuck out her bottom lip. "Okay. If I *have* to."

Dexter peeked at her through his eyelashes. She was so *cute* when she pouted. And she was so exceedingly wonderful. He thought that Megan truly was his other half – the extrovert to his introvert. The short time they had been married had been the best of his life. And, dammit, she *still* had that bottom lip stuck out!

Dexter felt a familiar stirring below his belt. He stood up abruptly and said, "Okay, I guess I've meditated enough."

Megan smirked.

On the fifth floor, Jessica Queen was reading the synopsis of the new blu-ray DVD movie she had purchased earlier. Jessica had a well-kept secret: she was a lifelong horror-movie addict. Although the movie was a few years old, Jessica was looking forward to watching *The Messengers*, starring Kristen Stewart. She had never seen it.

"How could I have let *this* one slip by?" she asked herself.

Jessica popped a bag of microwave popcorn. While it was popping, she changed clothes, putting on a sweatshirt and sweatpants. She padded barefoot back into the kitchen and got a diet cola from the refrigerator as she waited for the popcorn to finish.

Jessica Queen was the object of much speculation among the male employees of Justice Security. She had been the executive secretary for the partners until just a few months ago, when she accepted the offer of partnership. She chose to live in one of the smaller apartments on the fifth floor, saying that it was all she needed.

Jessica had never had a gentleman caller at her new apartment. And she seemed to express no interest in any of the male staff. So, naturally, speculation ran along the lines of "She's a lesbian...gotta be!" or "I bet she's married to some schmuck and they're separated...or he's run off and left her."

Actually, it was neither. Jessica *did* have gentleman friends, but on the rare occasions that she overnighted with one, it was always at *his* place. She knew better than to bring someone to *this* gossip hole. And she *had* been married once, when she was eighteen. It lasted a year, and she guessed they split more from boredom than from real irreconcilable differences. She supposed she had loved him, but she was sooo young then...how could she be sure?

Since then, no one had gotten close enough to her heart to claim it. It was just as well. Jessica was happy with her life, loved her work, loved her partners, and enjoyed answering to no one.

The microwave *dinged*. Jessica took her popcorn and diet cola into the living room, and fired up her movie, ready to spend her evening terrified.

TONY ARMSTRONG ARRIVED at *Wham* at seven thirty. His uniform was pressed and clean, his badge shiny, and his weapon gleamed in its holster. Justice Security grunts did not wear hats, and Tony's dark brown hair was acceptable.

Tony hated evaluations. To him, the very fact that an evaluation was needed implied that the grunt in question was not qualified to "wear the brown". The partners insisted, however, in giving each employee every break imaginable, in the hope that they'd become good security personnel.

Nice dream, thought Tony. *But, Jim Crowe is as good as gone. I should have fired him back during the Jackie Blue job, when Dexter dumped him on his ass for being a smart-aleck bastard.*

Tony walked to the front entrance, passed the long line of supplicants begging to be admitted to the club with only a glance, and nodded to the two bodybuilders manning the front door.

"Evening, guys," said Tony.

"Eve'nin'," replied one. "You're about thirty minutes late, aren't you?"

Tony nodded. "Yep, you're right. But it was all prearranged with your manager. I'm Tony Armstrong, from Justice Security. I'm in charge of the uniformed people, and I'm here to evaluate one of my employees tonight."

"I hope to God it's that damned Jim Crowe," said the second one. He pointed his finger at Tony. "If I catch that jackass out somewhere, I'll probably have to have the cops arrest him for assault!"

"Assault? Why?"

"For hitting my fist with his face so much!" Both bodybuilders started laughing uproariously. Tony smiled politely.

"Thank you for your input, guys," replied Tony. "I'll keep it in mind."

Tony passed the two and entered the club. As he opened the door, the pounding bass and synthetic drums beat a steady, loud tattoo inside his head. He walked to his post, unobserved by Jim Crowe, who didn't bother looking up from a book he was reading.

"You're late for your post," said Crowe. "I'm gonna have to report it to Tony. He'll want an explanation as to why you kept me from doing my job properly."

Tony began to feel the stirrings of anger. He still stood in front of Crowe, but now his look had become a glare, and he had crossed his arms. He made no reply.

"Well? I don't have time to wait while you make up an explanation. I need it now." His snippy tone indicated impatience with an underling.

"Let's get some things straight, *Mister* Crowe," said Tony.

Crowe looked up with an annoyed look in his eyes, and a smart remark on his lips. When he saw that it was Tony, his mouth snapped shut, and his face paled.

"*You* are not in charge of anyone at Justice Security. You are lucky that you have held a job with us as long as you have. If I want an explanation from someone, I will obtain that explanation myself. You are required to perform your duties as you have been instructed. No more, no less. You will *not* treat *anyone* as someone that is beneath you in their life station, and you will treat your co-workers as friends and equals. They might just save your misbegotten life one day." He leaned over the table used as a desk. "Are we clear on this, Crowe?"

Crowe gulped. He had not expected Tony to be partnered with him tonight. And, now, he was in trouble. *Damn Brandon – it's his fault!* To Tony, he said, "Yes, sir."

Tony straightened and nodded his head once. "Good. Now, let's see you do your stuff, please."

"Yes, sir," Crowe said again, as he reached for his clipboard. His hands shook.

Crap! What else can go wrong tonight?

RAY PRUETT WAS WALKING with Miriam and Steve.

"I see your point, Ms. Apple," said Pruett. "But I can't define 'popular' any more than anyone else. For example, why did Studio 54 in New York remain popular, and survive for so many years?" He spread his hands. "I don't know the answer, and I'd bet that no one else does. The public is fickle, and something can fade from popularity in the snap of your fingers. Ah, here we are." They had stopped in front of one of the private rooms. Pruett opened the door, and handed a key to both Miriam and Steve. "Please utilize this room as your base of operation tonight. You each have a key, and you can come and go as you please. This room is soundproofed, so that you may conduct interviews in a quiet area.

Your first drinks are on the house, and so is the room. I must attend to a few other duties, and I beg your forgiveness. Please enjoy the night." He left.

"Thank you, sir," said Miriam to Pruett's back. Pruett waved a hand to acknowledge the thanks, and disappeared. Almost immediately, the music began again with a steady beat. It was a DJ with prerecorded music tonight...no live band on weekdays.

Miriam looked at Steve, who shrugged. She shook her head, and used the key.

The door opened into the most plush, comfortable-looking room that either of them had ever seen. The room contained two roomy, soft couches, and two love seats, all upholstered with the softest microfiber material that either of them had ever felt. Steve sat in one of the loveseats – and "in" was the correct word, because he sank deeply into it – and breathed a huge sigh of contentment. The four pieces of furniture were loosely grouped around a central coffee table, and on the coffee table was a panel containing several buzzer-type buttons, each labeled for their intended use. One was labeled "waitress", another said "music", still another said "club". One was labeled "djay", and another was labeled "discreet medical". Miriam could only guess what that one was for...

Miriam closed the door behind her. When the door clicked shut, the silence was intense. She couldn't hear anything from the club itself.

"Oh, my God!" she said. "I haven't heard 'nothing' like this *ever!*"

Steve smiled and nodded.

Miriam looked at Steve, shook her head, and snorted in derision. "Come on, Couch Captain! Let's go find somebody to bring back to this sweet, silent hole and talk to them."

They left the room and entered the central part of the club. From the private rooms, as they entered, they walked onto a small balcony that surrounded a circular dance floor. In order to enter the dance floor, a customer would have to walk down two small steps, which were placed in several spots along the dance floor, allowing access from all sides. The DJ for the evening was perched on a small, circular stage one third of the way onto the dance floor, accessed by a runway that connected to the balcony. The balcony area had many small, square tables for club seating. The bar was also along the balcony, recessed into one of the walls. Three barstools were strategically placed in front of the bar in lieu of a table, but patrons were discouraged from sitting in them for very long. Two bartenders, dressed in polo shirts, with a red plaid vest over the shirts, were continually working. Demand for drinks, even on a weeknight, was high. Waitresses, looking slightly haughty and dressed in short dresses and black hose, effortlessly weaved in and out between the patrons, collecting payments and tips from the customers.

And, customers were in abundance. They were everywhere! You would think that it was Saturday night! On the dance floor, they were packed shoulder to shoulder, all gyrating to the beat of the music.

The music was deafening.

Miriam leaned into Steve, and shouted into his ear. Even so, he could barely hear her.

"Ready?"

Steve nodded.

They stepped down and joined the gyrating crowd.

"WHATEVER YOU SAY, SIR," the deputy mayor said to the mayor. *You brain-damaged prick.*

"Of course, whatever I say," said the mayor.

The mayor, Glenn Gould, had been pontificating again. This time, the subject had been crime and the recent influx of new crime in the city. Gould did not mention anyone by name, but Deputy Mayor Morris McIllwain knew who the mayor was talking about. Mickey Giambini and, God help them, Esteban Fernandez!

Mayor Gould leaned back in the car seat, gesturing with his right hand, while his left arm was around his trophy wife. "It just stands to reason, Morris. The police department is incapable of stopping any type of crime in this city. The only reason that the Gaimbini mob is somewhat tame right now is because the FBI is monitoring them from across the street! And what is our police department doing during all this? They're arresting prostitutes, ticketing traffic violators, and holding their hats and their hands out to any crime boss that offers them a dollar!"

"Ow! Gle-enn!" said the mayor's trophy wife, wincing at the pressure his hand was putting on her shoulder.

"Oh, I'm sorry, honey," said the mayor, moving his arm to his side. "Remember those dirty cops that kidnapped that kid a little while ago? A private gumshoe had to bust it up, with some FBI help! What's up with *that*, Morris? And I don't even want to *talk* about the Fernandez thing! Jeez, thirty thousand people could have been killed, *and our cops didn't know a thing about it!*" Gould started punching his fist into his hand. "We have *got* to get a handle on these things, and I mean *now!*"

Even though they had discussed these things many times in the last few weeks, Morris knew that unless the mayor cleaned house in the police department, nothing would change. The city would continue to be a joke to the rest of the state...Hell, the *country*...and there wasn't anything they could do about it.

"The only saving grace about that situation at the convention center was Joey Justice," replied Morris. "God only knows what would have happened if his security company hadn't been on top of things."

The mayor snorted in derision. "I have a couple of opinions about *that*, I can assure you. *And* Mister Joey Justice!"

I just bet *you do, you officious blowhard!*

The mayor's trophy wife squealed. "Oooo! We're *here!*"

The limousine had stopped in front of *Wham*.

Chapter 3

Louie opened the door at the Justice Security building and allowed Donna to enter the building first.

"You are *such* a gentleman, Louie," said Donna, with a smile.

"Why, thank you, Ms. Yarbrough," Louie replied.

Donna took his arm as they crossed to the front desk.

Mark Haase stood as they approached. "Good evening, Louie," he said, then looked at Donna. "And a good evening to *you*, Ms. Yarbrough. I've heard some good things about you." He looked significantly at Louie. "You can guess where I heard it."

Donna smiled demurely, while Louie tried to hide his obvious embarrassment.

"Anything going on that I need to know about, Mark?" asked Louie.

Mark shook his head. "No, Louie, it's a quiet evening," replied the desk man. He slid a folded piece of paper across to the partner. "That's tonight's panic word, sir. Just in case."

Louie took the sheet of paper, unfolded it, then slid it back to Mark. "Thanks, Mark, I got it." He turned to Donna. "Would you like a tour of the place?"

Donna smiled and looked enthusiastic. "Of course, Louie! It would be a genuine pleasure."

Louie beamed with pleasure. He turned to Mark and said, "Mark, we'll be wandering around the building, and then we'll retire to my apartment. If you need me, it better be a huge emergency...understand?"

Mark smiled. "I do, sir. Unless someone calls out the panic word, I won't be calling you."

Still beaming, Louie replied, "Sooo glad to hear it, m'man!" He held out a hand to Donna. "Ready?"

Smiling back at the big man, Donna said playfully, "Whenever you are, *Mis*-ter Washington!"

"Might as well start at the bottom and work our way up," offered Louie. "Then we don't have to backtrack."

"Good enough. Let's go!" said Donna.

Justice Security, Incorporated owned its own building on a tree-lined street in a better part of the city. The six-story aboveground edifice occupied a large portion of a city block, with parking areas for visitors, and a landscaped, park-like green area on its south side. The building itself was constructed of three-foot-thick reinforced concrete walls. Each window was made of thick bulletproof glass, including the visitors' entrance door. The building extended six floors underground. The bottom three underground floors were used as a vehicle storage area, and housed various armor-plated and bullet resistant vehicles to be used as protective equipment for transporting and defending employees or clients. The next underground level was the armory. All types of weapons were stored in the climate-controlled armory, from revolvers and automatic pistols, to mortars, to surface-to-air missiles and launchers, and various armor-piercing weapons. Enough weaponry and ammunition were stored in the armory to take down a small country's government, should they be hired for such a thing...and they had been, twice, under ultra-classified government contracts. The holding cells were also on the same floor as the armory, which caused some discomfort among new employees...until they met the people responsible for guarding any prisoners the company may be holding. The floor above the armory was records storage. This floor contained the paper files, computers, data storage, and research areas needed for executing and completing client contracts. The final underground level was the garage for employee parking, and was accessed by a ground-level entrance contained by a thick, heavy steel door embedded into the concrete walls of the building.

At ground level, the first floor contained the reception area, the cafeteria, building security, the new medical facility staffed by Dr. Orval Eugene Bishop, an M.D., and by Dr. Caleb Mitchell, a Doctor of Psychology, and visitors' rest areas. The second and third floors were occupied by employee offices, conference rooms, smaller meeting rooms, and clerical services. The fourth floor housed executive offices and the situation room. The fifth floor was for guest housing, and a few residential apartments. The top floor contained all residential apartments for the top level people of the company. The roof of the building had a helicopter pad, equipped with two armor-reinforced, stealth-equipped, black ops helicopters always ready to fly at a moment's notice. The company also owned two private jets and two large cargo planes, which were housed at a private airfield just south of the city.

Louie chose to ignore the four lowest levels of the building. He felt that giving away all of the company's secrets to someone he was dating would not be a smart thing to do...so, their tour began with the data processing sub-level.

"As you can see, this is the brain of Justice Security," he said. "We have resident nerds, geeks, and hackers all working to keep us up to date on the latest bugs, spyware, malware, and general data processing. I'm told that we have a computer setup that is actually slightly better than the one at the National Security Agency, and enough storage capacity to store all of the country's personal and financial records three times over, with the entire contents of the Library of Congress twice...and we'd still have room to store most other countries' records as well."

"Wow!" said Donna, wide-eyed.

"You remember my partner, Dexter, don't you? You met him a couple of weeks ago," asked Louie.

Donna nodded.

"He's in charge of this bunch of kids."

"I thought he was the martial arts master and teacher for the company," said Donna.

Several of the "nerds, geeks, and hackers" were working in some of the cubicles, since cyber-time doesn't know sunrise, sunset, midday, or midnight.

"He is...but he's a big computer geek, and an extreme hacker, too." Louie paused to wave to one of the workers. "His wife, Megan, was his second-in-command down here. They fell in love, and eloped...right after she was offered a full partnership in the company. She was responsible for pinpointing Esteban Fernandez' farmhouse just outside the city here, when we first butted heads with him, and led one of the two helicopters that tried to take him out. She got wounded in that farmhouse attack, and turned into Lady Rambo." He stopped and chuckled. "Ain't nuthin' excites that woman more than the chance of a firefight with some bad guys...except Dexter. And sometimes, I wonder which excites her more..."

"So you actually tried to take out Esteban Fernandez *before* the attempted attack at the convention center?"

"Oh, yeah. See, he said he was gonna kill us all anyway, and when it turned out that he was right outside the city..."

"A little...*pre-emptive*...strike was in order...correct?"

Louie nodded. "We thought we'd done him in, but he escaped...barely...and came back to try to take out not just us, but thirty thousand *innocent* people, too." He paused and took a deep breath. "Donna, there is evil in this world, small 'e'. Then, there is Evil, with a capital 'E'. And then there's the devil. And then there's Esteban Fernandez." He looked deeply into her eyes. "*That* scares me. And he's out to get us. He'll try again. I just hope we're ready. I don't *pretend* to hope to take him out...I just want us all to survive his next try."

"OKAY, JIM, YOU'RE LOOKING okay up here as far as procedure," said Tony Armstrong. "You still have a problem with your presentation. *Smile* at these people, Jim! They are the customers of *our* customer, and we have to treat them with professionalism and respect! Now, you did great with the mayor and the vice-mayor, but you could try sucking up just a *little* bit less."

Jim Crowe looked at Tony with anger.

Tony chuckled and held up his hands. "Joke, Jim, it was a joke! You handled him quite professionally. I'm proud of you."

Jim's feathers smoothed a little. "Thank you, sir. I appreciate that you noticed." Jim, truthfully, didn't realize that the mayor had just passed him by. Jim wouldn't have known the mayor if he'd come up and slapped him on the ass! But *Tony* didn't need to know that, of course.

"Okay, Jim, the big boss and his lady will be here anytime," said Steve. "I'm gonna go out onto the floor and find Brandon and Patty, and make sure that they're okay. You yell if you need something – that's what the radios are for, okay?"

"Yes, sir."

"Okay, back in a few." Tony strode purposefully into the club.

As Tony walked out of sight, Jim exhaled. He didn't even realize that he had been holding his breath.

BRANDON WAS GYRATING on the dance floor. He really wasn't dancing, per se…if the truth were known, he was trying to get away from the huge subwoofer he had wandered too close to before the music started. When the DJ, Icy Hot, took the stage, he gave no warning – he immediately started the music. Of course, like most clubs, the music was loud enough that a normal human couldn't hear his own voice even if he shouted, and Brandon felt his heartbeat corresponding to the bass beat of the subwoofer. And his head was corresponding, too. And it *hurt!*

So, he was gyrating out of the way, trying to dodge dancers that didn't seem fazed by the repetitive beat. And, naturally, he gyrated out of the way of the subwoofer – stepping on and bumping into several dancers - and found himself in front of one of the huge, six-foot-tall, regular speakers blasting out to the dance floor!

Brandon pressed his hands to his ears, and it helped a bit. He still couldn't move – the fire marshal's capacity limit for *Wham* was four hundred, and it seemed as if all four hundred people were crowding him into the speaker. He felt as if his brain was about to turn to jelly, when a hand fell on his shoulder.

It was Tony, who was taller than Brandon, and more stoutly built. As he led the younger man away from the speaker, people naturally parted and gave Tony plenty of room. Once they were at the other end of the "pit" area, Tony stopped and turned to Brandon. Tony mouthed something, but Brandon still couldn't hear him. Tony leaned close to Brandon's ear and yelled again.

"Where's Patty?" shouted Tony.

Brandon leaned toward Tony. "She *was* at the bar, sir!" Brandon shouted back. "I haven't seen her for a few minutes!"

Tony nodded and leaned forward once more. "I'll go look for her, son. Stay sharp…and stay away from the speakers!"

Brandon smiled at his boss and said, "Yes, sir!"

Tony patted Brandon on the shoulder and began making his way to the bar. Again, people made a path for the man without his having to say a word. Brandon shook his head in amazement, as he tried to move through the crowd.

"I GAVE YOU A TWENTY, asshole!" shouted the bar patron. "You're not gonna gyp me!" The patron, a stout man around six feet, began to reach toward either the bartender or the cash register with his right hand. The destination was unknown, because the hand never got there. A small hand grasped his wrist with a strength that belied its delicate appearance. The hand then turned the belligerent man's wrist backward and up, into the small of his back, while another hand pushed the back of his head with deliberate firmness onto the surface of the bar.

"Sir, I can break your arm...or I can escort you to a table. I can also escort you outside. The choice is yours," said a female voice firmly near his right ear. "But I saw the entire transaction...Jimmy, the bartender you just called an asshole, gave you the correct change. You gave him a ten. Now, I want you to make your choice. What do you want me to do?"

The man, astonished and in some discomfort, said, "Please let me up! I'm sorry! I won't cause any more trouble, I promise!"

"All right, I'll let you up now. Remember your word," admonished the voice.

The pressure on his head was removed, and his wrist released. The man stood, grabbing his right wrist with his left hand and rubbing it. He glanced at his captor. He saw an extremely attractive blond, approximately five feet two inches tall, wearing the two-toned brown uniform of Justice Security. His mouth fell open, but it was never determined whether the man was struck dumb by her attractiveness or the fact that she had stopped his belligerence with such ease.

Patty watched the man, bouncing and balancing on the balls of her feet. If the man chose to break his word, she was ready to "explain" things to him with harsher treatment, and then throw him out. If he honored his word, she'd ask Jimmy to give the guy a drink on the house...a *weak* drink.

The man continued to stare at her. Finally, he shook his head, turned away, and disappeared into the crowded dance floor.

"Thanks, Patty," said the bartender. "Dude was really looking for trouble."

Patty smiled at the bartender, who was kind of cute. "Just doing my job, Jimmy."

"And doing it really well, I see," said a familiar voice behind her.

Patty, surprised, whirled around to see Tony standing with his arms crossed.

"Good job, kid," said Tony. "Almost as good as Misty. A little more seasoning, and you'll be giving her a run for her money!"

Patty blushed and smiled shyly. "Thank you, Tony."

"You seem to be doing better than Brandon tonight," he replied. "Let me tell you what happened..." And he told her about finding Brandon trapped by the crowd in front of the speaker. Both of them started laughing.

"You should have seen him – you would have thought somebody was sucking his brain out through his nose or something."

"I'll have to tease him about it," said Patty. "So, how's the Crowe evaluation going, sir? I mean, it's none of my business, but if there's something I can do to help him, I'd like to know."

Tony shook his head. "At this point, he can only help himself, Patty. His job depends on him now."

Patty nodded. She looked down with a look of concern on her face.

Tony was surprised. "You genuinely care, don't you?"

"Yes, sir. So does Brandon. I know that Brandon complained about Crowe, but it was only because he didn't know what else to try with the man."

"You kids don't worry about him. He'll be fine, even if he doesn't keep his job with us. Joey will do everything he can to find the man something else."

"SWEET MEGAN...I HAVE to get up. I need to slip downstairs and check on that computer security program."

"You need to get *up*, all right, Dexter...stay here and check *my* program."

"Megannnn..."

"Mmmm...show me your hard drive, Dex..."

"...AND I *promise* the citizens of our city that my administration *will* do the right thing on that issue!"

"Thank you for those comments, Mayor Gould. Mr. Mayor, what do you think of club *Wham,* and why do you think it's so popular?"

"Miriam, *Wham* is a wonderful nightclub, and it has an innovative design. I think it's attention to the latest in music, lighting, and customer service will ensure that it becomes a permanent fixture in our city, for both residents *and* visitors!"

"Thank you for speaking with us, Mayor Gould."

"My pleasure, Miriam."

Miriam Apple looked at Steve. Steve eased the camera down and nodded to her. "Aaaannnndddd, cut. We're done." She turned to the fidgeting politician and repeated, "Thanks again, Mr. Mayor. I appreciate your comments."

The mayor, looking around at the private room, said, "Channel 7 paid for *this?*"

Miriam chuckled. "No, sir. Channel 7 wouldn't pay my *door fee*, much less a private room. No, the manager...what's his name, Steve? Oh, yeah Ray Pruett...*comped* me this room!"

"Wow," replied the mayor. "He must be a member of the *other* party...he didn't even *offer* me a private room!"

"AND *this,*" said Louie to Donna, as he opened the door to his bedroom inside his apartment, "is my bedroom."

Donna smiled demurely...and entered the room, pulling Louie behind her.

"SO...IS IT TO BE TONIGHT...or no?"

"No sign yet, sir."

"My patience is limited."

"I understand, sir, but it's beyond my control. I will advise when it happens."

"Very well. But, quickly, *amigo.* I cannot play these games forever."

Chapter 4

It was 8:45 PM.

"We are sooo late!" said Misty.

Joey just smiled.

Misty saw the smile and smacked Joey's arm. "Asshole. You just *had* to start that, didn't you? You *know* how I hate being late!"

"We're not late unless the boss says we're late," replied Joey. "And the boss says...we're not late." He pulled into the parking lot of *Wham,* and parked the car.

Misty giggled. "And Ray Pruett?"

"He can get over it," said Joey. "Or he can hire Jim Dandy's bunch." Jim Dandy was the owner of a competitive security company, and a former college buddy. Jim had a habit of showing up just in time to make Joey look like an amateur. "Ready?"

"Let's go," replied Misty, climbing out of the car. When she stood, she turned back and grabbed her purse from the seat. Her radio fell out onto the seat, but she didn't notice.

They moved toward the front entrance. As they approached, both noticed the line waiting to enter the nightclub stretched all the way around the building.

Adopting his best Cary Grant imitation, Joey said, "Look, darling – it must be terrible to be one of the little people!"

Misty played right along, adopting Audrey Hepburn's walk and talk, replied, "Yes, it certainly is, dear. What shall we do in the Hamptons this season?"

The couple began laughing and walking toward the front door, hand in hand...the perfect example of a young couple completely in love with each other.

They came to the velvet rope, and the muscular bouncer with the radio headset stopped them. "We're pretty full tonight, folks...looks like the wait's gonna be a while."

"We're expected."

"Yeah, I've heard that before." The bouncer pulled out his clipboard. "Name?"

"Joey Justice," said Joey quietly. "Misty and I are up in the security rotation."

"Sorry, Mr. Justice," said the bouncer. "I should have recognized you. Come on in." He unfastened the velvet rope and held it open. Lots of catcalls and angry shouts of "Hey!" came from the line behind them.

The second muscleman opened the front door for the couple, and, as they entered, the man with the clipboard and radio headset spoke into his microphone.

"They're here, sir. They both just went inside." He paused, listening. "Yes, sir. Standing by." He waved to the other man. As he came close, the first one said, "Be ready...Pruett says the shit is about to go down."

INSIDE THE ENTRANCE, Joey paused to nod at the hat-and-check girls, and asked Misty if she wanted to check her bag, knowing that her gun wasn't in it. Misty declined, and they walked on to the security checkpoint.

Crowe was alone. Tony was still circulating on the floor inside the club.

"Good evening, sir...ma'am. How are you tonight?" greeted Crowe.

"We're fine, Jim. How's it been tonight?" replied Joey.

"Very quiet so far, Mr. Justice."

"Jim, what's the panic word?"

Crowe looked around to make certain that they weren't overheard. "Jitterbug, sir."

Joey nodded. "Good."

Misty was looking through her purse. "Aw, crap!"

"What's wrong, honey?" asked Joey.

"My radio...it isn't in here. It must have fallen out in the car."

"I'd be glad to retrieve it for you, ma'am," said Crowe.

Joey smiled. "Not this time, Jim – you're on duty in here. We're plainclothes." To Misty he said, "Want me to go?"

Misty smiled at him. "I'm a big girl, Joey...I'll go. Be right back."

"Okay," replied Joey. "Hey, if you don't mind, I may go on ahead and look for Tony. I'd like to have a word with him."

Misty had turned to go back to the car. "Go ahead – I'll find you." She headed toward the door.

"Well, Jim, time to earn our money. If I miss Tony, please tell him to stay here. I need to talk to him."

"Yes, sir."

Joey climbed the five stairs and disappeared into the club.

"IT'S CONFIRMED, SIR. They're here."

"Ah, it is acceptable, Pruett. You may begin."

MISTY NOTICED THAT the two musclemen were not in sight as she walked across the parking lot to the parked car. She wondered why they had abandoned their post...they were supposedly the first line of defense at the front door. Well, what the heck – they weren't *her* company's employees. Jim Crowe would just have to pick up the slack.

She came to the car, inserted her key, and unlocked the passenger door. Sure enough, there was her radio, on the seat of the car.

Before she had a chance to lean into the car to retrieve her radio, a couple of nondescript vans pulled up in the front of the club, and another van stopped at the employees' entrance. The doors to the van flew open, and at least twenty men, all carrying what looked to be Uzi machine guns, ran into the front of the club. Ten or so more, also well-armed, ran through the employees' entrance.

"I don't friggin' believe it," Misty said to herself. She reached into the car, grabbed her radio, and pressed the 'transmit' key. "Mark! This is Misty! *Jitterbug! Jitterbug!*" She watched as she transmitted the message as what appeared to be sheets of solid steel quickly lowering over the front door, and the second story windows. She began running toward the employees' entrance, still shouting into the radio. "I just saw approximately thirty heavily armed men enter the club, and now steel plates are lowering over the front entrances!" She came to a stop just before reaching the employees' entrance. A steel plate was lowering over that way in, too. "Check that, Mark! Steel plates have lowered over *all* of the entrances! Every window, every door is covered by steel plates! Send all the partners to *Wham*! Call Marcus Moore and get the FBI in on this! Do you copy, Mark?" She released the 'transmit' key and was immediately rewarded with a high, shrill shriek. "*Dammit!* They're jamming the radio signal!" She had no idea how much of what she had been saying got through!

Bastards have my man in there...they have no *idea what they've done!*

Misty dug into her purse for her cell phone. When she brought it out of her purse, there was no service, and the screen was wavering. *Oh, God, can I* please *catch a break? What are those bastards* not *jamming?*

She began running in an attempt to find an open convenience store...or even a pay phone.

It was 9:00 PM.

AT JUSTICE SECURITY, Mark Haase did hear part of the transmission.

Mark's radio was on the front desk at the building's entrance. Mark had just stood up, plastic plate from home in hand, and was about to walk to the microwave.

"Mark! This is Misty! *Jitterbug! Jitterb*—" And the radio began a shrill squeal.

Mark, not expecting trouble, dropped his food. He sat down in his chair, picked up the shrieking radio, and depressed the 'transmit' key.

"Misty, please repeat your transmission."

SQUEEEEEEEAAAAAALLLLLL!!!

Mark turned the radio down, picked up his phone, and dialed Misty's cell phone.

"The customer you are trying to reach has turned off their phone or is in a non-service area. Please try your call again later."

Mark hung up his phone and sat for a moment, thinking...although, he really didn't have a choice. He reached over and pressed the one button on his console that he had never seen pressed in his five years on the job – the button someone had jokingly labeled, 'Panic'.

THE SIREN WAS LOUD. Jessica jumped up from watching her horror movie, heart pounding a mile a minute, when it went off. She assumed a defensive hand-to-hand stance, and whirled toward the front door when the recorded voice began speaking.

"THIS IS NOT A DRILL! THIS IS NOT A DRILL! THE ALL-ALERT HAS BEEN SOUNDED AT THE FRONT DESK! ALL EMPLOYEES WITHIN THE BUILDING REPORT TO YOUR ASSIGNED DEFENSIVE POSITION! ALL PARTNERS WITHIN THE BUILDING REPORT TO THE FRONT DESK! THIS IS NOT A DRILL! REPORT TO YOUR DEFENSIVE POSITION AND AWAIT ORDERS!"

Jessica's eyes widened. She knew about the 'panic' button, of course, but had never heard it...and she also never expected it.

But she knew one thing: All hell had broken loose for that alert to sound!

She quickly pulled on some jeans and grabbed her handgun. As she pulled her jeans up, her mind was whirling.

Elevator or stairs? Wonder what's happened? Have we been invaded? Jeez, I sure hope nobody's hurt – since Louie got shot in the arm a little while ago, and Charlie got shot in the leg, and that sweet Jennie Lou died, I don't think I could take another death in the family. Elevator or stairs? Hmmm...I think stairs are in order this time.

Jessica eased her front door open, checked both ways, and eased into the hallway. She pulled her apartment door closed behind her and made sure it was locked. Then she made her way carefully to the stairwell.

"DON'T ARGUE WITH ME, Donna! This is serious! You *stay* here, and you keep the front door locked, you hear me?" said Louie forcefully. "Until I know what's goin' on, I want you *safe!*"

Donna, sitting up in Louie's bed, had the covers pulled to her chin. Her eyes were wide, but she nodded. "Okay, Louie. Please be careful."

Louie looked at her and his expression eased a bit. "Only way I know to be, babe." He cocked his semi-automatic and headed to the door.

"LET'S *go,* Megan! Let's *go!*" said Dexter. Dexter had pulled on a t-shirt and sweatpants, and picked up a sword and a few throwing stars. He was beside the front door of their apartment, ready to go.

"I'm coming, Dex," called Megan. She walked into the living room, dressed in denim shorts, and a cropped t-shirt, carrying a semi-automatic rifle in one hand, and an Uzi machine gun in the other. Over her shoulder, she carried a small pack containing ammunition clips for both weapons, along with a few odd surprises. A folded bandana was tied across her forehead to hold her hair back from her face. "Okay, honey, I'm ready." Then she smiled.

Dexter shook his head and eased open the door.

"Oh, *please,*" said Megan, who kicked the front door wide and strode purposefully from the apartment. She went down the hall to the elevator, which opened immediately. She climbed aboard, and looked at her husband. "Coming, dear?"

Shaking his head at his know-no-fear wife, Dexter eased into the elevator. "Megan, you could at least *pretend* that danger is right outside our door."

The elevator doors slid shut.

IN THE LOBBY, APPROXIMATELY 30-35 employees were milling around the front desk. There were members of the support staff, like cafeteria workers, uniformed grunts, and a couple of plainclothes people. Dr. Caleb Mitchell, the Justice Security staff psychiatrist, who had been working late on some case files in the medical area, was also there. All were armed, and ready to defend the building as needed.

Mark was explaining to Dr. Mitchell what was happening, when the partners appeared in the lobby. They saw everyone surrounding Mark's desk, and walked toward it.

"Hey!" shouted Louie. Immediately the room was quiet. "What's going on, Mark?

"Wow," said Mark. "I'm sure glad to see *you* guys!" He took a breath. "Misty used the panic word. From the nightclub."

"So, did you confirm?" asked Dexter.

"No, sir," replied Mark. "This is what comes across the radio on her frequency." He turned the volume up so that everyone could hear the shrill shriek. He turned it down after a few seconds. "I then tried calling her on her cell phone. No service."

"In the middle of the damn *city?*" said Louie. "No way."

"I got the same thing from Joey's cell phone, sir," Mark said. "I tried it right after I hit the panic button."

The partners all thought for a moment.

"And neither one has checked in since?" asked Jessica.

"No, ma'am," replied Mark. "I also tried the radios assigned to Tony, Crowe, King, and Ferguson. All of them have the same squeal on that frequency."

"What do you think, guys?" asked Dexter.

"Well, something is wrong, obviously," said Megan. "But the question is, *what* is wrong? How do we respond? With flashers, sirens, and loaded guns, or with quiet and stealth?"

"You're right, Megan," said Louie. "But, it was the panic word. We all agreed when we set it up that we come running when we hear it." To the crowd gathered around the desk, he said, "Listen up, people! Here's what we're gonna do..."

The phone on Mark's desk rang. Everyone looked at it.

Mark picked it up. "Justice Security, Mark Ha—..."

"Mark, this is Misty. Did you get my transmission?"

"I got the panic word, but that was enough, Misty." Louie was gesturing to Mark to hand him the phone. "Hold on, Misty, Louie wants to talk to you." He handed the phone to Louie, who had come behind the circular reception desk.

"Misty, baby, what has Joey done now?"

"Nothing like that, Percy. Here's what happened..."

Louie interrupted her. "Wait a minute, I want to put you on speaker phone. Everybody in the building is right here. It might save time." He pressed the button that fed her call through the hidden speakers under the desk.

"Okay, Misty, go," said Louie.

"Here's what happened...," she said, then told the story. "...and *something* is jamming every signal within several blocks of that club!"

"You're on the ground there, baby," said Louie. "What do you want us to do?"

"Here's the list," she replied. "Better write it down."

Mark produced pen and paper.

"Ready, Misty."

"First, call in every unassigned or off-duty grunt and plainclothes we have and send them to me at *Wham*. Second, call Marcus Moore. Tell him what's happened, and ask him to meet me at the club, too. Third, I need Megan."

"I'm here, Misty."

"Great! Remember that list of supplies we talked about a couple of weeks ago? When we fantasized about taking down another building, like we did Giambini's building?"

"Of course I do!"

"Put it together and bring it with you. Louie, you might also call Dr. Bishop and Caleb. We don't know what's happening inside that club, and there may be injured people. Caleb can provide first aid if Dr. Bishop is busy."

"This is Caleb, Misty. I'll take care of that for you, and we'll see you in a few minutes."

"And I guess we need a partner on base in the building. Jessica, do you mind?"

"Glad to, honey. And don't worry – we'll get Joey out of there!"

"Oh, Jessica, I don't know what I'll do if we don't!"

It was 9:20 PM.

Misty hung the phone up and began jogging back to the club. *It's been twenty minutes...what's happening inside that club?*

Chapter 5

Jim Crowe was lying on the part of the floor above the dance pit usually reserved for the DJ, or live band, if one had been appearing. His leg was bleeding below the knee, but not as badly as it had been. Crowe didn't know if it had slowed because he was running out of blood, or if it had just begun to finally clot. His leg was broken from the impact of the bullet, however, and the pain was excruciating when he moved his leg.

Ray Pruett was standing beside him, working with the equipment left in place by the DJ, who was now lying dead under the table that held the turntables.

Crowe had no idea where the others were. They had disappeared like wisps of smoke from a distant fire. He didn't question that, however. It made sense to him. A child's rhyme ran through his mind then: *Run away, run away, and live to fight another day.* He had no doubt that all the rest of the security personnel assigned to the club tonight were probably still in this room with him, and were all probably able to see what was happening right now.

They were hiding, awaiting opportunities.

There wasn't much happening at all right now.

Oh, there had been a huge flurry of activity at nine o'clock, when the guys with the guns had come in and immediately shot Jim in the leg. Jim was, naturally, a bit fuzzy on details after that happened. He had been aware that one of the swarthy men had taken his weapon from its holster. And he had known that his radio didn't work, either...something was jamming the signal. He figured out that some of the shouting and screaming sounds he had heard earlier were the men taking over the dance pit.

As things quieted a bit, one of the men came back and dragged him closer to the pit, and then dropped him. Jim guessed that they wanted to keep an eye on him. He saw several people herded into the pit. He assumed they were the people from the private rooms.

One was speaking rather loudly.

"I'm the goddamn *mayor* of this city! You *will* take your hands off of me!"

There was the sound of a thud, a slight scream from the lady with the speaking man, and the man suddenly couldn't walk very well. One of the gunmen had hit him in the face with the butt of his gun.

Crowe also saw Miriam Apple as she was herded into the pit.

On the runway, the music had stopped, but the DJ was still behind the equipment.

Ray Pruett came out on the runway. He shot Icy Hot in the head.

Jim was shocked. He could have heard a pin drop...it was that quiet.

Pruett flipped the switch for the microphone.

"Please remain calm," he told the crowd. "I don't want to kill any of you. Correction: any *more* of you." He giggled to himself then, a mad, uncomfortable laugh...as if he was lying, knew it, and knew you knew it, and didn't care. "Also, please be quiet...I have to set up something here, so that all of you can hear...won't be a minute." He began to work on something that no one could see. "Oh, and would one of you gentlemen please bring *that*..." and he pointed at Jim Crowe, "...out here with me? Thank you."

One of the men had dragged Crowe out onto the runway and dropped him close to Icy Hot's body.

Pruett was still adjusting the equipment, then stood straight. "Got it. Can you hear me, sir?" he said into the DJ's microphone.

"I can," said a voice on the other end...through the sound system.

"All *right*," said Pruett. "Ladies and gentlemen, my name is Ray Pruett. I'm the manger of this establishment."

IN THE CROWD, MIRIAM nudged Steve, who had kept his digital palm-sized movie camera hidden in his pants pocket...until now. Steve already had the camera rolling. He winked at Miriam, who nodded and turned her attention back to Pruett.

"I'd like to introduce all of you to the owner of *Wham*...even if it is by telephone," he continued. "Sir, you're on."

FROM HIS PLACE IN THE crowd, hiding his face and weapon, Joey was listening intently.

"Allow me to introduce myself," said the voice. Joey's blood turned cold.

Oh, God! I know *that voice!*

"I am indeed the owner of this club," continued the cold, emotionless voice. "I've spent a great deal of money on this club for just this one night."

Joey was holding his breath, and didn't realize it.

"For just this one opportunity to catch my enemies, Joey Justice and Misty Wilhite. You see, *senors y senoritas,* I am Esteban Fernandez, and I am going to kill *Senor* Justice tonight."

I am in some serious *shit!* thought Joey.

MIRIAM LOOKED AT STEVE and whispered, "Oh, no...not again..."

DEPUTY MAYOR MORRIS McIllwain's thoughts ran along the same lines, but were much more graphic. He looked at the mayor, and his thoughts were definitely *not* sympathetic.

You happy asshole, you *got us into this! If you had cracked down on crime earlier, and helped Joey Justice instead of listening to the Police Commisioner's crap, we might not be here!*

Mayor Gould, still dazed from the blow on his head, was rolling his head and muttering. His trophy wife had her arms around him, and she gently shook him every few seconds, trying to revive him.

As if he's going to be any help. McIllwain looked around the room, trying unsuccessfully to spot Joey Justice. *If anybody can bail us out of this mess, it'll be Justice.*

WHEN THE GUNMEN HAD burst into the room, Patty saw immediately that they were outnumbered. She dove into the crowd, and thanked her lucky stars that she had decided to go all out when she got dressed for tonight's assignment. She took off the almost-tan uniform shirt. Underneath, she had worn her best shirt-dress – the one with the spaghetti straps. And, just in case, she had worn a pair of matching shorts under her uniform pants...which she also had taken off and discarded.

Her weapon was in its hiding place...Misty had taught her a few things, like where to hide her weapon...and her radio.

Now, hiding among the crowd, she blended in. It gave her a little freedom.

Patty had never heard Fernandez' voice, but it chilled her to the bone. She unconsciously looked for Joey as she listened to the drug cartel leader speak. She hoped he had hidden well, and she hoped he stayed there. Let she and Brandon take care of this one...with Tony's help, of course.

"I, OF COURSE, DO NOT wish to hurt any of you," continued Fernandez. "I only wish to have those two brought to my manager. When that is done, I will open the doors again, my men will go away, and you will be free to go."

Many of the people in the crowd knew Fernandez was lying. They remembered how this dangerous criminal had been willing to kill thirty thousand people at the city's convention center, just so that he could kill the Justice Security partners. They remembered that Joey Justice, along with Jim Dandy, had averted that catastrophe by seconds. So, they knew he was probably lying, and would have no compunctions about killing all of them.

Others in the crowd knew nothing about that incident. They had only fuzzy impressions that Esteban Fernandez was not a nice guy...perhaps something they had heard from their neighbor, or somebody from the bus route, or in the grocery line. Those people were not aware of the danger posed by the insane Mexican drug cartel leader. But they knew Joey Justice, and they knew he was a standup guy. So, in their minds, whatever this man wanted with Joey had to be bad.

Only a handful of people didn't know either man. As a result, they were indifferent to what was going on, as long as it didn't affect them.

A couple of the people close to Joey had recognized him. By nudging and giving each other silent looks, finally six to seven people moved, not as a group, but in ones and twos, around Joey, mostly blocking him from view. One girl had moved to his side. She gently ran her finger over his hand to get his attention. When Joey moved his eyes to look at her, she pointed to the floor with the same finger with which she had touched his hand. After a few moments, he got the idea, and squatted down. The group immediately moved in closer to him, giving him the opportunity to crawl away unnoticed. Joey, however, didn't move at first.

He took inventory of what he had on him...a small can of Mace, a couple of knives – one strapped to his leg, one in a sheath between his shoulder blades – and two handguns. His Glock was under his sport coat, behind his belt in the small of his back. The other gun was a Phoenix Arms .25 caliber Raven, in an ankle holster. He also had a six inch, sand-filled leather sap.

Nothing explosive. Joey regretted that slightly, but figured that it was probably for the best, given his accidental history with things that explode.

Now, where could he go?

He was in the pit with all the other people in the club. He couldn't possibly crawl out unnoticed without being spotted, so leaving the pit was out of the question.

There were no tables to hide under in the pit.

Joey was feeling desperate. He *had* to find a place to hide! He needed to think for just a few minutes...to try to think of a way to save these people from Fernandez, because he knew that nothing was ever what it appeared to be when dealing with that mad bastard...

Wait! Joey hit on an idea of a place to hide...right here in the dance pit! It would be soooo obvious, but it felt soooo right!

Joey started crawling to the only place to hide that was open to him...

BRANDON, TOO, HAD IMMEDIATELY shed his uniform shirt when the gunmen had burst in. He had also unclipped most of the security trappings from his belt and slid them along the floor. His Glock went inside his front pants pocket...the holster was discarded. He untucked the tail of his "wife-beater" blue t-shirt. He pulled the gold chain out from inside the shirt, and let the pendant that Chris had given him hang in the center of his chest. He now could pass for one of the patrons.

He could see Crowe, bleeding and looking pathetic...but, somehow...he also looked...*noble?* Jim *Crowe?*

He stood quietly, waiting for Fernandez to continue speaking...and dreading it as well.

"AND, SO, *senors y senoritas,* here we are: will one of you tell my men where to find Joey Justice and Misty Wilhite?" continued Fernandez.

Silence from the crowd.

"Can any of you provide me with the location of any of the Justice Security people in the building tonight? Other than the one lying next to my manager, of course? *Por favor?*"

More silence from the crowd.

"Very well. *Senor* Pruett?"

Pruett snapped to attention. "Yes, sir?"

"You may proceed with the piece of trash on the floor in front of you," said Fernandez.

Pruett's eyes didn't just widen...they sort of bugged out as he smiled slightly. His head turned to Crowe. "Thank you, *Senor* Fernandez, you are most gracious."

As Pruett moved to Crowe, Fernandez continued speaking.

"This is directed to Joey Justice," he said, through the speakers. "What happens next is on your head, *senor.* When you and Miss Wilhite turn yourselves in to my men, this will all stop."

Pruett took out a pair of pliers.

"The last time you spoke with my man Pepino, Justice, you applied a pair of pliers to one of his testicles." Crowe's eyes widened when he heard this. "I can do no less than my opponent."

Unnoticed by Crowe, four of the men circling the pit had approached behind him. They each took on of Crowe's limbs and held them securely against the floor. Crowe winced in pain as his bullet-shattered leg was moved.

Pruett moved closer, and unfastened Crowe's pants. Pruett moved the pants down until Jim Crowe's groin area was naked, and his manhood exposed to the audience. Crowe's eyes were so wide, it seemed as if he didn't have any eyelids at all...and they never left the pliers held in Pruett's hand. Crowe's head began shaking left and right, slowly at first...then more frequently. As the pliers touched his scrotum, Crowe could not keep quiet any longer.

"No! NO!! *NOOOOOOAAAAAAAHHHHH!!!!*" Crowe's cries turned into screams as the pliers snapped shut, destroying his right testacle.

"Where are they?" shouted Fernandez. "Tell me where they are, and the pain will stop!"

Crowe's screams had turned to a low moan. He mumbled something to Pruett, who was grinning into Crowe's face. Pruett was enjoying his work.

But, what Crowe told Pruett caused Pruett to lose his smile.

"What did he say, *Senor*?" asked Fernandez.

Pruett gulped. "He said that only Joey Justice was inside the building. Misty Wilhite had returned outside just before the shutdown."

Silence poured from the speakers.

Finally, a calm, quiet voice came from them. "*Senor.* Are you telling me that your flytrap only caught...*one* of my flies?"

Pruett, eyes downcast, only nodded.

"Would you like to tell me how you can bring the *puta* to me if she is not even *in the building?*" Fernandez began speaking calmly, but ended in a shout. "*yeeeeeeaaaaAAAAAAHHHH!*" came shrieking through the speakers, along with the sound of furniture crashing and glass breaking, until, finally, the noises abated. Hard breathing could be heard...then Fernandez returned.

"Pruett," he said.

Pruett said, "Yes, sir."

"Kill that brown-suited *hijo de puta. Kill him now! You men, shoot him UNTIL I TELL YOU TO STOP! NOW!*"

The four men who had moved onto the platform to hold Crowe's arms and legs aimed their machine guns at Crowe and began firing. All four had emptied their magazines before the shooting stopped. The screams and crying from the crowd were drowned out by the sound of gunfire, but gained in volume as the shooting ended.

What remained of Crowe resembled raw hamburger.

As the crowd's noise dwindled to a few quiet sobs, Fernandez spoke again.

"Joey Justice. I know you can hear me, *senor*," he said. "You have one hour to surrender to my men. You will not be harmed...for a price. You will be allowed to speak to Misty Wilhite. You will convince her to come inside the club, and to surrender to my men.

"When she is inside, you will both be brought to me, and these people will not be harmed.

"However...at the end of this hour, if you have not surrendered, my men will execute one of these people every fifteen minutes, until you *do* surrender.

"We will speak again at the end of the hour, Justice. If you have any kind feelings toward the patrons of this club, you will surrender."

It was 10 P.M.

No one in the audience had any more hopes about getting out of the club alive.

Chapter 6

Outside, a good-sized crowd had gathered, centering around the parking lot of *Wham*. Several private and company cars from Justice Security surrounded the parking lot. Two ambulances, both from private companies and now on the security company's payroll, were on site, called in by Caleb Mitchell. Dr. Orval (please call me Buddy) Bishop stood next to one, and Dr. Mitchell was next to the other. On the street, five police cars had stopped. The first police car had stopped. The cop found Misty, and asked what was going on. The other four cars each contained cops that were backing up the first one. Louie had arrived, and was standing beside Misty with his arms crossed and a huge scowl on his face. He was trying to look intimidating to the cop.

Misty was trying with increasing frustration to explain to the cop that this was a private affair, and that it would become a Federal operation as soon as Marcus Moore arrived. The cop continued to argue with Misty that she needed to clear her people out of the area, and that the cops would take over from this point on.

Finally, Misty said to the cop, "Fine! If you want to take over, take over! But my people aren't going anywhere. If you're so convinced that I don't know anything, why don't you walk up to the front door and ask politely if they will let the hostages go?"

The cop nodded. "That's step one, Miss Wilhite."

She bristled. "It's *Ms.* Wilhite, officer. And if you'd like to have a small something to remember me by, just say the word!"

Louie unfolded his arms and took Misty gently by the arms. "Don't lose your temper yet, Misty...this guy ain't worth it." To the cop he said, "Mister, I don't know where you were taught public relations, but I can see it didn't take. I just saved you from a strong lesson in civility."

The cop looked from one to the other. "Are you threatening me?"

Louie smiled. "No, officer, I'm not."

"But *I* am, hot shot," said Misty. "My fiancé is inside that building, threatened by armed men, and you're playing games with me!" At the word "fiancé", Louie's eyes widened and he looked down at Misty. "That's fine, you have a dick, and I don't. But, I assure you, the man with the biggest dick will be here in just moments, and you *will* wish you had listened to me!"

The cop nodded. "That's *it,* lady! You're under arrest! Obstructing a police officer in performance of his duties, disobeying an official order, and resisting arrest!" He took his handcuffs from his belt and said, "Are we gonna do this easy, or do I get to rough your pretty face up a little?"

"How about choice number three, dickface?" said a voice from behind the cop. "That choice is that I give her a free shot at you!"

The cop whirled around to face the voice, and found himself staring at an FBI badge.

"Hi. My name is Marcus Moore, and I'm the man with the biggest dick. You fine examples of what officers *shouldn't* be have just been assigned to me by your Chief. That means you follow my orders *to the letter.*" Marcus folded the leather wallet containing his badge and put it back into his jacket pocket. "Hi, Misty...Louie. Let me have a couple of more minutes with this *great* example of the city's finest, would you?" He turned back to the cop. "Do you have anything else to say right now, Officer Dickface?"

The cop, whose face had turned beet red from anger, swallowed. Hard. "No, *sir.* I don't have anything else to say, *sir.*"

"Yes, you do."

The cop looked into Marcus's eyes defiantly. "Oh, yeah? What would that be, *sir?*"

"You are to apologize to Ms. Wilhite."

The cop shook his head, his eyes never leaving Marcus. "Not happening...*sir.*"

Marcus took a step forward until his nose was only a millimeter away from the cop's nose. His voice could barely be heard. "You sure about that, buddy? Think *hard*...your job...heck, your *freedom* from being arrested...depends on your answer."

"*Arrested?* What are you talking about?" The cop backed up a step.

Marcus pointed to Misty. "Ms. Wilhite is a duly appointed agent of the Federal Government, performing her duty as she sees fit. You are preventing her from performing that duty. I could arrest you right now, and you know what the charges would be." He put his arm down. "So...what's your answer?"

The cop finally gulped. He turned to Misty. "I apologize, Ms. Wilhite."

Marcus smiled. "Thank you, Officer...?"

"Hollingsworth."

"Got a first name, Hollingsworth?"

"Stanley."

"Good, Officer Stanley Hollingsworth. Now, to show Ms. Wilhite that you are indeed sorry for your attitude and threats, you are to work by her side. You will perform anything she asks you to do." He moved again into the cop's face. "Do we...understand...each other?"

"Yes...sir."

Marcus pulled back from the cop's face, and turned to Misty. "We have reports that the Mayor and Deputy Mayor are also inside."

"Oh, that's just great," she replied.

"Mayor Gould isn't a big fan of Justice Security," said Louie. "Marcus, you remember that case that your friend worked on? The one with the kidnapped kids and the dirty cops?" He looked at Hollingsworth.

"Sure, I do," said Marcus, as he thought, *The one that Madeline made herself known...how could I forget that one?*

"We heard rumors," added Misty. "We couldn't confirm them, but the rumors said that the Chief and the Deputy Mayor were clean, but that the Mayor welcomed any 'contribution' that came his way."

Marcus nodded. "We heard that, too...but we couldn't confirm them. Not with anything to charge him with, anyway."

"I need to know who's behind this," said Misty. "Then, I can decide just what we need to do to end it." She looked at Marcus. "Is it my case, Marcus?"

Marcus nodded again. "It is, Misty. I will back you with all the authority of the United States Government, but the case and its decisions are all yours." He gave a sidelong glance to Hollingsworth. "I hope everyone involved understands that."

Dexter and Megan came up to them then. "Sorry it took so long. Megan had a lot of stuff to put together in the armory."

To Misty, Megan said, "It took most of the back of one of the minivans to bring what we talked about."

Misty nodded. "I thought it might. We'll have some fireworks tonight." She said to Dexter, "Can you gather our employees together? Also, any cops that might be around, too. We need to try a few things."

"Sure can," said Dexter. He moved off.

"Oh, and one last thing," said Misty, as she whirled around to face Louie. Her outstretched hand smacked Hollingsworth on the right temple. He fell to the ground heavily and didn't move. He was unconscious.

It all *appeared* to be an accident. Marcus snickered behind his hand, and Louie laughed out loud. Megan's grin was as wide as a jack o'lantern.

"Oops," said Misty.

SECURE IN HIS HIDING place for the moment, Joey wiped a frustrated tear from his eye. He was mouring the death of Jim Crowe, who had died so indignantly at the hands of Justice Security's mortal enemy.

Joey had opened up both his radio and his cell phone. As far as he could tell, both were in working order. The signal was jammed somehow, which told him that this plan had been in place for quite some time, maybe since they had last encountered Fernandez during the Championship boxing match.

On the speakers, Fernandez spoke. "Pruett. We must speak. Please take me off of the speakers."

Joey couldn't see him, but he assumed that Pruett jumped to do what his employer told him to do, because he could no longer hear Fernandez. He could hear Pruett speak occasionally, but it was too low to make out what he was saying.

I have to think! How can I get these people out of here without getting them killed? And where in the world are my people? Thank God that Misty went out when she did!

THE PRETTY BLONDE WITH the light freckles across her nose moved up behind Brandon slowly and cautiously. Brandon's attention was focused on

Pruett, so he did not notice her. When she was within arm's reach, she touched the small of his back. From the way he jumped, she knew she had frightened him. She grasped his arm as he whirled around, and put her finger to her lips.

"Patty!" said Brandon, whispering through his teeth. "You scared the *crap* out of me!"

"Shh!" Patty replied, whispering herself. She cupped one hand over Brandon's ear as she whispered into it. "I know where Joey is hiding. I saw him go there."

Brandon whispered back. "Where?"

Patty whispered Joey's hiding place into Brandon's ear. His eyes widened as she told him.

"You gotta be kidding!"

Patty shook her head.

"Incredible! I never would have thought of it!"

"Me, either," said Patty.

"Do you know where Tony disappeared to?" whispered Brandon.

Patty nodded.

"Where?"

She smiled at her best friend. "Look around, Brandon. Look closely, and *observe*. He's in plain sight. You'll see him."

Brandon looked at her quizzically, then began looking around the room. He gave himself over to what he called "observation mode". When his mind was focused on this mode, he noticed almost everything. As he studied each face in the crowd, his mind registered everything that his eyes saw. After a few minutes, he was positive that he had not missed Tony.

He shook his head as he whispered to Patty, "He's not in sight anywhere in the crowd."

Patty smiled. "That's the crowd. Look somewhere else."

Brandon began scanning the room, and, indirectly, his captors. As his head passed around the room, it stopped...then it returned to one particular spot.

The guard directly across from him wore sunglasses and a baseball cap, as many of the guards did, and held his submachine gun easily in his hands. As Brandon noticed the man, the man reached up, slid his sunglasses down a tiny bit, and winked at Brandon.

The guard was Tony Armstrong.

"I will be tee-totally damned!" whispered Brandon in awe. As he winked back, Brandon was thinking furiously. "Patty."

"Hmmm?"

"Tony's all alone up there...he can't do much by himself."

Patty nodded. "I know...not without getting himself killed."

"He needs one of us up there with him."

"How?"

"I'm thinking...and I have an idea!" He bent closely to here and began to whisper in her ear.

"That just might work, Brandon! We can try, anyway!"

"Okay, people, listen up!" shouted Misty above the murmurings of the crowd around her. "First order of business: we *have* to get our communications back. That means we have to find what is jamming them, and neutralize it. Dexter, can you put your people on it? Coordinate with Marcus, please. Maybe the FBI has some equipment that we don't."

"We're on it, Misty," replied Dexter. He gestured to several people around him, and they moved away from the crowd. Marcus waved to Misty and moved to join them.

"Next, I really need someone to move up to one of the entrances and take a close look at those doors. We need to know what we're dealing with, and how hard it would be to get past them. Maybe there's a lock of some sort that we could try to get past. Ideas?"

Louie waved to Misty. "I can do that. I'll take the four cops that are awake. We'll check it out." Louie spotted Charlie Li across the crowd. "Charlie! Hey! Come with me, man!" Louie's group moved off toward the entrance.

A balding man with a slight paunch around his middle made his way to Misty.

"Ms. Wilhite!" said the man. "Could I speak to you for a moment?"

"I'm very busy, sir. Please make it quick."

The man nodded. "My name is Tim Wilson. I'm the producer for Channel 7's news broadcasts."

"I have no comments for the media, Mr. Wilson. I wouldn't know what to comment *on*."

Wilson shook his head. "I'm not here for that. I think...no, I'm *sure* that Miriam Apple and her cameraman, Steve, are also inside." He took a breath.

"And it's *my* fault that they are. I want to get them out of there. What can I do to help?"

Misty looked at the man's eyes. "Are you serious?"

Wilson nodded. "I am. The entire news department is available to help you, if you need them."

She smiled and shook her head in disbelief. "Wow." She pointed to the direction that Dexter's group moved toward. "You know Dexter Beck?" The man nodded. "His group is over in that direction. They're concentrating on breaking this jamming that's going on. Will you help them?"

Wilson ran a hand over his head. "On my way, Ms. Wilhite. Thank you." He began jogging toward Dexter.

"Wow," said Misty again, in disbelief.

Raising her voice to the crowd, she shouted more instructions. "I need my grunts to take over crowd control, please. Move around the parking lot, and anyone that isn't Justice Security, police, FBI, or medical and emergency personnel need to be at least fifty feet or more away from the building...civilians, please cooperate with our uniformed and emergency people..."

LOUIE AND HIS GROUP had moved over to the main entrance to the club. They stopped a few feet from the steel door. Louie crossed his arms, then began rubbing his chin as he studied the setup.

"Mr. Washington," said one of the younger cops.

"Um-hmm," replied Louie, deep in thought.

"I bet that door isn't very thick."

Louie put his arms down and said, "What makes you think that?"

"Well, if it was much more than a half-inch thick, wouldn't it be a little too expensive for a nightclub?"

Louie shook his head. "I don't want to take anything for granted in this situation. My friend is in there, along with a lot of VIPs...No, we're going to be cautious. We don't even know who's behind this yet."

The cop, eager to show that he *could* be helpful, moved close to the door, then rapped on it. "Oh, wow," he said. "It's really thick. Somebody spent some money on this thing!"

Many changes that were built into this building were specifically designed by the owner, in this case, Esteban Fernandez. The steel panels that had closed off the building from the outside were only part of the design changes. The main entrance doorway, for instance, was recessed inward, away from the outside wall. This was to allow room for the placement of several small doors around the door facing. These doors were monitored and controlled by security cameras, computer, and a series of interlocking infrared beams. When the beams were interrupted for a period of several seconds...about the time it takes to knock and speak a sentence or two...the computer would trigger an automatic pre-programmed response.

As the young, eager cop spoke the last sentence in his previous comments, the doors surrounding the entrance opened, and what looked like metal tubes sprang out of their hiding places behind the small doors.

The metal tubes were gun barrels.

The tubes began firing from every angle around the door: left, right, above, and below. The cop was dead before he realized that he had triggered a booby trap, and his remains resembled Jim Crowe's inside the club...like so much hamburger meat.

Louie's mouth was wide open in shock, and Charlie Li's eyes looked wide enough to pop out of their sockets. The remaining three cops were in various stages of shock, and the crowd in the front of the building had become silent.

"*Fuck* ME!" shouted Louie. "Everybody get the fuck *away* from any doors on this building right *now! GO!*" he said, as he pushed a cop with one hand, and Charlie Li with the other.

Misty had begun running toward the entrance as soon as she had heard the shooting. She stopped when she was standing beside Louie.

"Oh, my God!" said Misty. Quietly, she said, "Who has this kind of money, Louie? Who would do this?"

"I got my suspicions," he replied.

"Me, too," she said. "I'm thinking Mexican..."

"So am I," replied Louie. "But it ain't no taco salad I'm thinkin' about!"

Dexter and Megan came up to them.

"We found the scrambling signal. It was fairly simple," said Dexter.

"We neutralized it," said Megan.

"Good," replied Misty. "Louie and I were having thoughts about who has enough money to pull off something like this."

"Oh, I think it's Fernandez," said Dexter.

Misty and Louie looked at him.

"What makes you say that, Dex?" asked Louie.

"That's easy," he replied. "The trap was sprung *after* both Joey and Misty had gone inside the club. If Misty hadn't come back for her radio, she would have been inside, with Joey. Fernandez is the only enemy we have that has a huge hard-on for both of them...in different ways, of course."

"Yeah," agreed Megan. "He wants *you,* Misty, and he wants you alive...for a while, anyway. Joey? Well, he wants Joey dead, but not until his spirit is crushed. Whatever he has planned for you would crush Joey's spirit easily...to the point that he wouldn't care if he lived or died. Fernandez would then kill him, and enjoy it."

"So," said Dexter. "It's gotta be Fernandez. He's the only one that has the money *and* the motivation."

"Easy enough to find out," said Louie. "If the jamming is gone, call Joey on his radio."

Misty took a deep breath. "Okay, here goes." She lifted her radio. "J-2 to J-1, do you read?" She paused, listening for a response. "J-2 to J-1, do you read?"

They all listened intensely. Finally, Misty's radio received a whispered response. "Shh! You'll give him away!"

ALMOST LOST AMONG THE murmur of the crowd, the sound of Misty's voice on her radio registered with Patty. She grabbed Brandon's arm and pantomimed speaking into a radio. Realization hit him. As his eyes widened, he nodded to her, and moved to block her from view as she dropped to a crouch and retrieved her radio.

The volume on her radio was very low, but she could clearly hear Misty as she called for Joey again.

"Shh! You'll give him away!" she whispered as a response.

"Patty?"

"Yes, it's me."

"How is everyone? How is Joey?"

"I hate to report this, Misty, but we have a casualty...it's Jim Crowe. They shot him to pieces."

"Oh, no! Patty, *who* shot him to pieces?"

Patty paused. "Esteban Fernandez' people shot him. They were trying to find out if Jim knew where you and Joey were hiding. They tortured him, and when they found out from him that you were outside, and that he didn't know where Joey was hiding, Fernandez lost his temper, and had his men shoot Crowe with their Uzis until their magazines were empty."

"So Fernandez is in there?"

"No! He's talking through the sound system, as if he's somewhere else...maybe on a phone somewhere. Pruett definitely belongs to Fernandez, though. Pruett's the one that tortured Crowe."

"What else can you tell me?"

"There are twenty to thirty men with automatic weapons – the weapons are Uzis. They're surrounding the dance pit, and most of the patrons are in the pit. Tony Armstrong has taken cover as one of the guards, and Brandon and I are trying to come up with a way to join him. With three of us posing as guards, we should be able to do something."

"Patty, you said 'most of the patrons'...what do you mean?"

"Well, I saw Miriam Apple and her cameraman earlier, but I haven't seen them for a while. A few others, too. But I'm sure they're here somewhere – maybe just out of sight. And, Misty?"

"Here, Patty."

"The mayor and the vice mayor are in here, too. This could be tricky."

There was a moment or two of silence. Finally, Misty spoke.

"And Joey?" she asked hesitantly.

Patty smiled as she responded. "He's fine, Misty. He's got a safe hiding place, and we're going to do what we can to keep it that way. But, what about the patrons? Most of them are the same age as Brandon and I...maybe even a bit younger. We can't let them die!" *Or the rest of us, either...*

"Patty, you guys do what you can to help those people, *but don't get caught!* We'll try to figure out a way to help you from out here."

"Will do, Misty."

MISTY'S EYES WERE FOCUSED on some far-off spot on the horizon, as she slowly lowered the radio to her side. Her emotions were whirling inside her.

Megan came to Misty's side, and she put her arm around Misty's shoulder. "He's okay, hon...he's okay. That's all that matters right now, isn't it?"

Still staring, Misty said, "Is it?"

Megan, concerned, replied, "Well, of *course* it is! We'll get those people out of that club, and Joey will be back in your arms in no time!"

"Will we?" Misty mumbled. "How? The whole place is booby-trapped, those people are inside, at least two people are dead...I would really like to hear some ideas right now! I mean, I know what I *want* to do, but I don't know if this is the time."

Marcus chose that moment to ease through the crowd, and stopped at Misty's side.

"Misty, I think it's time we tried a standard FBI tactic. I'd like to shut off the electricity to the club now."

Misty looked into Marcus' eyes. "Marcus, do you really think that would be safe? I mean, a cop just got killed when he and Louie knocked on the door, for heaven's sake! And, we have confirmation that our old friend, Esteban Fernandez, is behind all of this. So, I don't know if shutting off the electricity would trigger something even more deadly. I think we should leave it alone for now."

Marcus looked down as he thought about it. "You're probably right. We sure don't want to do anything that risks more people."

"That's all mighty fine," said Louie, "but we still don't have any ideas on how to open that place up!"

Chapter 7

Tony Armstrong stood on the edge of the dance pit, aiming his Uzi at nothing in particular. He was wondering what would be the best way to get Patty and Brandon up on top with him.

Earlier, Tony made a quick decision when he saw the first armed men running into the dance area – he ducked into the bathroom. He went into a stall, stood on the toilet, and moved a ceiling tile out of the way. He then boosted himself up into the ceiling and moved the tile back into place.

He had no sooner let go of the ceiling tile when he heard the bathroom door slam open. An accented voice shouted, "Come out! Come out now!" Apparently, no one was in the bathroom.

Tony heard the stall doors slamming open one by one, then the same voice said, in Spanish, "*No one is here. Gringos must not piss very often!*" Two voices laughing, then the bathroom door closed.

Tony eased his way along the ceiling joists toward the air ducts. He intended to follow one until he could locate a place that he could ease through down to the floor. He was within a few feet of one when he spotted something that made him freeze, and gave him a momentary panic.

It was a security camera. An expensive one...and the only reason that Tony had seen it when he did was that it had moved its lens from side to side, scanning the length of the air duct.

After a couple of minutes, Tony decided that the camera had not seen him. He backed up a couple of feet along the way he had come, and then continued at a right angle. He hoped that he was heading toward the private rooms.

Inch by inch, Tony maneuvered. With very little light, he peered carefully around as he moved, watching for more security cameras. He dared not disconnect any of them until he knew for sure what was going on, and who was behind it. After that, it would be up to him and his co-workers, along with Joey, to neutralize the situation.

Slowly, careful to make no noise to betray his passing, Tony came to what he believed to be the private rooms. The ceiling tiles had changed, becoming thicker and better insulated. Once the tiles changed, he moved a few feet further along.

He could see no cameras within a few feet of his position. He had no way of entering the the room beneath him without brute force – he would have to kick a tile down into the room. He wasn't worried about being able to do the job...his biggest worry was sound. He wasn't concerned about being heard within the private rooms, but being heard along the ceiling outside of the private rooms. Well, risk was part of the job, whether it was when he served in Afghanistan years ago, or here in the city. He positioned himself, braced against the joists, then kicked downwards on the tile. On the third kick, he had an opening large enough to slip through.

Dropping through his newly made hole, Tony noted that he was inside one of the private rooms. His sense of direction had not failed him. The room was deserted.

He quietly worked his way to the door, grasped the knob, and turned it with great ease, then, very gently, opening the door the tiniest bit so that he could get a glimpse of the club outside.

All of the club patrons seemed to be in the pit. Several armed men stood around the edge, weapons pointed into the crowd. Jim Crowe was lying on the runway, and it looked like he was bleeding from a wound on his leg.

At that point, Tony heard a voice over the sound system identify itself as Esteban Fernandez. Tony realized that it was time to take action. He reached into his pants pocket and pulled out a quarter. Opening the door about six inches, Tony tossed the quarter through the gap. His aim was perfect – he hit one of the men standing around the pit with the quarter! Tony ducked inside the room, getting ready.

After a moment, the door was swung open a bit by a gun barrel. Tony, ready for anything, grabbed the weapon's barrel and pulled the surprised guard inside the room. Tony hit the man twice as hard as he could, once on the temple and once on the Adam's apple. Dazed and choking, the guard dropped the Uzi and clutched his throat. Tony grabbed the man's head and chin, and twisted. There was a loud snap, and the guard's neck was broken. Tony eased the door shut.

The guard was about the same size as Tony. He began stripping the dead man as quickly as he could. Removing his own uniform, he dressed in the guard's clothes. *Cool. An almost perfect fit!*

Tony dragged the guard's body to the private room's bathroom and propped it up on the toilet. He hid his uniform under the sink, and looked at himself in the mirror.

With the sunglasses, he looked like an Hispanic thug.

Showtime! he thought, as he headed for the door and opened it. He walked over to the pit, and took his place in the circle. He glanced at Crowe over on the runway, but something had happened while he was killing the guard, and Crowe was dead.

Don't think about it, Armstrong! Later! Right now, these people need you!

Scanning the crowd, he spotted Patty and Brandon immediately. He also spotted Joey squatting on the floor behind a group of people. Inwardly, he smiled as he watched Joey crawl to his hiding place, open it up, and then pull it closed behind him. Good. Let Joey be their "ace in the hole".

Meanwhile, Patty had spotted him. He used a series of hand gestures, specialized by Justice Security, telling her to come to Brandon and wait for instructions.

MIRIAM APPLE SAID, "Mr. Mayor, let me make sure I understand you." She glanced at Steve to make certain his camera was picking up the conversation. Steve nodded to her. "You say that Joey Justice is the reason that Esteban Fernandez has declared war on the city?"

"What I'm saying, Ms. Apple, is that Esteban Fernandez is likely a respected businessman," replied Mayor Gould. "He seems to be trying to open legitimate businesses in our city – this club, *Wham,* or even Pinky's Limousine Service – which have both been abruptly interfered with by Joey Justice and Justice Security!"

"So you're implying that Justice Security was involved with the explosion at Pinky's Limousine?" asked Miriam.

"That's *exactly* what I'm saying!"

"And what proof do you have, Mr. Mayor?"

The mayor started to say something, but stopped. "I'm...I'm working on it right now."

"And how, exactly, is Justice Security responsible for tonight's violence here at club *Wham,* sir? As near as I could tell, they were only supplying security...hired by the club's manager."

The mayor hesitated again. "I'm not sure, but I know it to be true, Ms. Apple."

Miriam eyed the mayor for a moment. "How's your head, sir?"

"Oh, my head is okay...hey! What are you implying? Get *away* from me!"

"One last question, please, Mr. Mayor," said Miriam.

"What *is* it, Ms. Apple?"

"The DEA has labeled Esteban Fernandez as a violent leader of a Mexican drug cartel, and the FBI has said that Fernandez is a violent criminal looking to expand into the United States by force if need be. Doesn't that make your statements blaming Justice Security for the violence performed by Fernandez rather...absurd? And does it perhaps indicate that your administration is giving credence to the rumors stating that you are on Fernandez' payroll?"

The mayor glared at Miriam, realizing that he had been maneuvered into a corner stating exactly what she had implied. "This interview is *over*, Ms. Apple."

"But could you just answer the question, sir?"

"Ms. Apple, I not only will *not* answer, but I will see to it that you won't ever share these accusations!"

PATTY FERGUSON AND Brandon King watched as Tony gave them instructions. Both nodded.

Patty, with Brandon shielding her, whispered into the radio. "J-1, this is PF-1. I know you can hear me, so press the transmit button twice to let me know I'm getting through."

She pressed her ear to the device, and heard two clicks.

"We all know where you are. Tony is in a position that helps us, and he says that you need to stay there. You are our "ace in the hole". Do you understand, sir?"

Two more clicks.

"Great. Stay frosty, and pay attention, sir!"

Suddenly, Patty's arm was grasped tightly from behind. She almost dropped the radio, but, instead, drew back her hand as if to hit the person that grabbed her. She stopped when she saw who it was.

"Lady, if you know where Joey Justice is, send me to him. The mayor has just admitted on camera that the rumors about being on Fernandez' payroll are true, and he has assured me that I won't survive to tell anyone," said Miriam Apple. "A reporter hates to admit it, but I'm frightened."

"LADY, I DON'T GIVE a flyin' fuck *who* you are, I am *not* leaving my man on that stoop like a piece of fuckin' *garbage!*" shouted the police chief. "It ain't *right!*"

"No, it isn't right, Chief!" shouted Misty with equal determination. "It's not right that he's dead, it's not right that there's a building full of people trapped by a crazy man, and it's not right that my fiancé is one of them!" She put her index finger on the chief's chest. "But, if you want to go get your man, by all means go *get* him! But I'll see to it that nobody comes after your body, either! Don't you *get* it, Chief? Fernandez has done all of this! Every bit of it! And we're stuck one jump behind him trying to keep him from another huge killing spree!" She waved at the club. "And we can't even get *in!*"

"Well, I know all that!" shouted the chief.

Megan called out to Misty. "Misty! Patty's trying to get you on the radio!"

"What the hell?" said the chief. "This ain't social hour!"

"She's our contact inside, you idiot! Why don't you shut your cockholster for a while, and pay attention?" She picked up the radio and keyed the transmit button. "PH-1, this is J-2. Were you looking for me?"

"I sure *was!*"

"Sorry. I was arguing with our illustrious chief of police."

"Keep him close, Misty! He needs to hear this! So does Mr. Moore!"

Misty spotted Marcus in the milling crowd and motioned him over. The chief had never left Misty's side. She looked in Megan's direction. Megan turned her finger in circles, indicating that the transmission would be recorded.

"Okay, Patty. I have them both here with me."

"I have Miriam Apple. She has something to say."

"Put her on, Patty."

Click. "Misty?"

"Hello, Miriam. What's happened?"

Miriam repeated what she had told Patty a few minutes earlier.

The chief just closed his eyes and shook his head. Marcus gave a cynical chuckle, and Misty rolled her eyes, thinking *What* else *can go wrong?*

"We copy, Miriam. We will act on your information as soon as we get you out. Meanwhile, you and Steve stay with Patty and Brandon...they'll take care of you until *we* can. Okay?"

"Thank you, Misty. And, by the way, I believe the vice mayor is clean."

Misty smiled. "Thanks, Miriam. Now, give the radio back to Patty before you guys give yourselves away!"

Misty whirled on Marcus and the chief. "We have *got* to get inside, gentlemen! And I mean *now!*"

"WOW," SAID MIRIAM. "Now I gotta pee!"

"I don't think they're taking...," started Brandon. He snapped his fingers. "*Wait* a minute! I've got an idea!"

"What?" asked Patty.

"Watch," said Brandon. He turned toward Tony and made sure that he had Tony's attention. As Brandon formed the hand signals explaining his idea, Patty started smiling and Tony started nodding.

"You're a genius, Brandon!" said Patty.

Tony replied to Brandon, who nodded.

"Tony says we can only go one at a time," he said.

"No problem," said Patty. "I think Miriam should go first, since she really has to go."

"I agree. Miriam, make some noise. Please direct it to Tony, so that he can be one of the guards that helps."

Miriam looked confused. "What the *hell* are you two talking about? Tony who?"

Patty laughed. "Oh, that's right...you don't know. Do you know Tony Armstrong from Justice Security?"

"The guy at the front desk, right? Yeah, I know him."

"Look up, at the edge of the pit."

Miriam looked up. Tony again lowered his sunglasses and winked, this time at Miriam.

"Our idea is that Tony needs help up there, and we have to find a way to get up there without attracting attention. We need to gradually take the place of several of the guards until we're all up there," explained Brandon.

"Since you have to go to the bathroom for real, and you're known for being pushy in your job as a reporter, you go in the first group," said Patty.

"And take the place of one of the guards," finished Brandon.

Miriam looked at both of the security personnel. She couldn't believe what she was hearing. "You're kidding, right? It's a joke. Gotta be."

"No, ma'am," replied Brandon. "No joke."

Patty gave a half-smile. "Welcome to Justice Security, Miriam. Nice to have you aboard!"

Miriam looked from one to the other, until she realized that they weren't kidding. Turning her head determinedly, she marched toward the edge of the pit. "Ohmygodi'mreallydoingthis..." Tony, and the guards on each side of him, turned their weapons toward her as she strode to the edge. "Hey! You! I gotta pee!"

No response from the guards.

"Are you *deaf*, or do you only speak 'Stupid'? If I don't go to the bathroom in just a couple of minutes, I'm going to leave a puddle on this floor!"

A guy in the crowd said, "Yeah, I could sure use a piss break myself, you know?"

"Me, too," said another guy.

"I can use a bathroom break," said a young woman.

Miriam turned to look up at Tony. "So, how about it, Mr. Bad-to-the-balls? Do we get to go or not?"

"Hey!" shouted Ray Pruett, still on the phone.

Tony looked toward the manager standing on the runway.

"Start taking them...just a few at a time."

Tony nodded and looked to his right and mumbled in Spanish. The guard on his right nodded, then motioned to Miriam and four others that had gathered around. They climbed the stairs out of the pit. Tony arranged the group, making sure that Miriam was last in line. He nodded to the other guard, indicating that the other man was to lead the way.

Arriving at the bathroom, which just happened to be the bathroom that Tony had entered to escape the gunmen, neither the guard or Tony said anything to the group, but the guard went first into the bathroom. Each person in line ahead of Miriam went inside, one at a time. Miriam hoped that she was doing what Tony wanted her to do – when her turn came to go to the bathroom, she balked.

"I am *not* going in there and taking a piss in front of either one of you!" she said sternly. "I won't be the one giving you your jollies!"

The guard, hearing Miriam's voice, opened the door to see what was wrong. Tony pushed Miriam into the guard, and followed the staggering, off-balance pair inside the bathroom. Tony pushed Miriam out of the way, then drove his fingers deep into the guard's Adam's apple. He found himself wishing he had a knife – it would be *so* much easier! Instead, he twisted the guard's head backwards until he heard the neck snap.

Miriam swallowed a gulp. Tony helped her up from where she had fallen.

"Great job, Miriam!" whispered Tony. "Not only are you a good reporter, but you are one *hell* of an actress!"

Stammering, and returning the whisper, Miriam replied, "Th-th-thank you, Tony." She pointed to the guard. "Is he...?"

"Dead? You bet your sweet ass. Want to help me undress him?"

She took a step back, fear showing on her face. "Uh-undress him?"

"Sure. You gotta put on his clothes to take his place. And we gotta hurry!" Sensing that Miriam was drifting away from him, Tony said, "Don't you need to pee?"

"Pee?" she replied distantly. Then, she snapped back to herself. "Yes, I do. I won't be a minute." She stepped into a stall and did her business. As she finished, she spoke. "If you'll pass me his clothes, I'll begin dressing."

Smiling, Tony said, "Sure thing, Miriam!"

Two minutes later, Miriam stepped out of the stall. The dead guard's clothes weren't a perfect fit, but they would pass casual inspection. Tony took the man's cap and put it on Miriam's head, tucking her hair underneath. He stepped back to look at her, moving his head up and down. Finally, he nodded.

"Needs one small finishing touch," he said. He handed over the guard's sunglasses, which Miriam put on.

"Good enough," said Tony. "Now, Miriam, we've been in here for a while. When we walk out of here, we have to look like two guys that just took advantage of the TV news lady, okay? We have to strut like we just blew our loads, and left the pretty news lady dead in the stall. Can you do that?"

Surprised at Tony's blunt talk, Miriam answered boldly, "I can do that."

"Good. 'Cause we aren't out of this yet. I'll take the lead, and you bring up the rear."

Tony opened the bathroom door, and stepped out, gun pointing up in his right hand, straightening his trousers with his left. The remaining four club patrons were watching him, and barely noticed Miriam...but they noticed that the two guards were alone. Their imaginations did the rest.

The patrons went willingly to the pit. Patty bounded up the steps as part of the next group. Tony motioned for Miriam to take her place along the pit, and spoke quietly to another guard, asking if the other man would assist with the new group. Miriam noticed that the new guard was about the same size as Patty. She looked down into the pit, and saw Steve looking up at her. Patty and Brandon had obviously found the cameraman and filled him in on the situation. She wondered if Tony planned to bring Steve up with them.

Oh, dear God, I hope we can pull this off!

Chapter 8

M egan entered the final code into her wireless controller, and looked at Misty.

"Ready?" Megan asked.

Misty looked around. Everyone was safely away from the front door of the club. She looked at Dexter, who shrugged. She looked at Louie. He nodded. She looked at Marcus. He nodded.

The receiver at the other end of the wireless controller was attached to an ugly, 5x7 pale grey brick of C-4 explosive compound. The brick had two silver bands on each side, wrapping around the explosive package. Upon reception of a signal from the controller, the receiver would pulse electricity into the brick of explosive. It would then explode, hopefully giving access through the thick steel doors of the club.

The events leading up to this attempt were shocking, and drove home the urgency of finding a way into the club.

Misty had been in the process of talking over and implementing a plan, when her cell phone rang.

When she answered, she said, "Misty Wilhite."

The voice that responded caused her to shudder.

"Hello, *Senorita* Wilhite. I hope you are enjoying my little trap."

She hurriedly waved at Dexter to get his attention, then pointed to the phone, mouthing, "It's him!" Realization hit Dexter, and he grabbed both Megan and Marcus and pulled them toward the electronic area to attempt to trace the call.

"Let's just say it has my attention, *Senor* Fernandez," she replied into the phone.

Fernandez laughed. "You realize that you were supposed to be examining the club from the *inside*, don't you?"

"Yes, I'm well aware of that."

"Fifty-seven minutes ago, I spoke to all of the people inside – not in person, of course – and told Joey Justice that he had one hour to turn himself in. He would be given opportunity to speak with you to convince you to come inside. If he chose to help, I promised that I would release the people inside.

"If he chose not to take advantage of my offer, then I told him that I would execute one of the patrons every fifteen minutes until he did surrender." Fernandez paused. "You are patched into the interior sound system of the club, and have been since the beginning of this call. Everyone inside can hear you." He paused again. "You have one minute. Please convince him."

Misty, taken by surprise, could only say, "You *bastard!* How do you live with yourself?"

"Quite comfortably, I assure you."

"Joey. Stay where you are. We've got an army out here, and we'll get you out. All of you. Please, stay calm. We have the FBI, the city police, every Justice Security agent available, and lots of television news folks. We're all working to get to you. Please don't give up hope, because..."

Fernandez interrupted her. "Joey Justice. Your time is up. *Senorita* Wilhite, you may listen, but you will not be heard as we continue." There was an almost inaudible *click.* "*Senor* Pruett, you may proceed. No, not that one...or that one...*yes!* That one!"

Misty could hear sobbing. It grew louder.

"Yes, *Senor* Pruett. Bring her onto the catwalk. What is your name, girl?"

More sobbing, then SMACK!

"Your *name, puta!*"

"Tr-Tr-Trudy. Trudy Hickerson."

"*Gracias, senorita.* It is nice to know the name of the one you are going to kill," Misty heard Fernandez say. "Pruett? Please shoot her."

Misty eyes widened as she heard the sobbing grow louder, and "no! please!", then BANG!

Misty heard silence.

"*Senors y senoritas,* she is but the first to be killed because Joey Justice has not made himself known to us. There will be another in fifteen minutes. Will it be you?"

The *click* of a disconnect on her phone.

Misty had slowly lowered the phone. She didn't realize it, but she was close to going into shock. She didn't give in, however. She reached down deep into herself and found some reserve strength.

Oh, Joey, may God have mercy on us all.

Misty took a deep breath. "*Megan! Louie! I need you!*" she shouted.

"OHMYGODOHMYGODOHMYGOD," said Miriam to Tony. "Why did they shoot that poor girl? Tony, *why didn't we stop them?*"

"Miriam, don't you even *think* about losing it right now!" said Tony under his breath. "There are three security people up here, four if you count Joey on the floor! And we have you and Steve...and you've got weapons, but neither of you have been proven under fire! We are outnumbered far too much right now to even think about making an assault! That's why we didn't stop them – we'd be dead right along with that girl!"

"ohmygodohmygodohmygod," continued Miriam quietly.

"Miriam! If you're going to lose it, go down to the pit before you do, so you don't give the rest of us away!"

Miriam shook her head. "No, Tony. I'll be fine."

Tony studied her a moment. "Okay. But if you start losing yourself again, I'll throw you into the pit myself. We can*not* afford to be caught right now. Do you understand?"

She nodded.

Steve eased over beside Tony, and whispered into Tony's ear.

"The *Gulf? You?*"

Steve nodded.

"See any action?"

Steve nodded again, then whispered again to Tony.

"You're kidding, right?"

Steve rolled up his shirt sleeve and showed Tony his Navy Seal tattoo.

"Steve, I apologize, man. I thought you were another TV geek."

Steve waved his hand to indicate that it didn't matter.

Tony nodded at Miriam. "Watch her, will you?"

Steve nodded.

"PEOPLE, MAY I HAVE your attention, please?" said Mayor Gould. "Right around me, please...yes, I just want to speak for a moment...thank you."

A small group of people had begun surrounding the mayor, many of them still in shock from the young girl's casual death, some of the women still sobbing slightly.

What is this voracious windbag up to now? Deputy Mayor McIllwain found himself standing next to the mayor. *This better not be some kind of self-serving grandstanding, or I'll hit him in the head myself!*

"What you have just seen happen can be directly tied to Joey Justice," started the mayor.

McIllwain stared open-mouthed at Gould, not believing what the man just said. Cries of "you dumbass!" and "what the hell are you saying?" were shouted from the group of people around him.

"I know it's hard to believe, but it's true," said Gould, over the cacophony coming from the small crowd. "Listen to me! It's true!" Gould began waving his arms in small circles. "Look at this club! It's a very successful business, and now it's been ruined because of Joey Justice! Esteban Fernandez is only trying to open businesses in this town...trying to help the local economy...trying to help families support themselves by providing jobs!"

"But wasn't this club built specifically as a trap to catch Joey Justice?" asked someone from the crowd.

Gould paused for a moment. "No! It was built to keep Justice *out!* He keeps trying to stop Fernandez from establishing businesses in our city! He has some kind of obsession with Fernandez, so *Senor* Fernandez tries to keep away from Justice."

"But, Joey Justice didn't shoot that girl...that Trudy girl," said someone else from the crowd. "Fernandez' people did that."

"But he didn't come out from his hiding place to save her, either," said Gould. "If he was innocent, he would show himself, and proudly!"

A man in the crowd shook his head. "You're wrong, Mayor. I wouldn't show myself, either, unless I could stop the killing somehow. This Fernandez guy is going to kill us all, whether Justice shows himself or not. You won't ever convince me otherwise."

As the mayor was about to respond, another voice chimed in. "Yeah. You won't convince me either...traitor."

Gould whirled to the voice just in time to be punched hard on the jaw by Vice Mayor McIllwain.

"Glenn, I believe I would stop talking now, if I were you," said McIllwain.

The small crowd around them began applauding.

THE SUBJECT OF THEIR discussion, Joey Justice, sat inside his hiding place, silently crying strong tears for the dead girl.

"HE ISN'T USING A CELL phone. At least, not one that we can detect," said Dexter.

"So we can't jam him the way he jammed us earlier," said Misty.

"Actually, we think we can," replied Megan.

"Or, at least, have a little jamming noise coming in while he's talking," said Marcus. "Make it a little tougher to hear what he's saying, maybe."

"It'll take time, though," added Dexter.

"Which we don't have," said Misty quietly.

Dexter nodded. "But," he said, "we figured out that Fernandez is tapped into the security cameras inside the building. It's how he sees, and how he was able to choose which girl to kill."

"We can block that, no problem," said Megan.

A glimmer of hope and a slight smile crossed Misty's face. "Do it." She turned to Megan. "Did you bring everything we talked about?"

Megan smiled. "Oh, yes."

Misty smiled back. "Then I need to talk to Louie."

Marcus gestured toward the front of the club. "I think he's with the city police, still studying the entrance."

Misty looked at Marcus. "Join me?"

Marcus smiled. "Sure."

They began walking toward the big man.

BACK AT THE JUSTICE Security building, Jessica Queen was sitting at the front desk with Mark Haase. She had nothing to do.

Even Mark had something to do. He answered the occasional incoming phone call from off-duty personnel that had answered the emergency summons. He told them what was going on, and directed them either to specific errands or to the *Wham* parking lot. He also monitored reports and security feeds from on-duty personnel at various posts through the city and the country.

Since the return of Fernandez, the building was on lockdown, and on red alert. While only a skeleton crew of personnel remained at the building to enforce security, they were backed up by non-essential personnel, like kitchen and janitorial crew.

Jessica estimated that only twenty or so people remained in the building.

It seemed empty.

And haunted.

She wished she hadn't watched the first two-thirds of her horror movie earlier. Now, she was creeped out in her own home.

Mark was good company, and gave her the illusion that she was doing something.

Jessica realized that she was keeping Mark from doing things that he might need to do, so she decided to go back upstairs to her apartment. She rose, told Mark good night, and told him to call her immediately if something happened. Then she headed for the elevators.

The doors slid open on the fifth floor, and the first thing Jessica saw was one of the in-house guards sprawled on the floor about five feet from her. It wasn't until she was beside the body that she realized that the body was in a pool of blood.

Jessica held her gun ready with her right hand, and turned the body over with her left.

It was Jeff Breeden. His throat had been cut, and cut so thoroughly that his larynx and windpipe were cut almost in two. His jugular had been sliced, so that he would have bled to death before he could smother from the cut windpipe. His face was a sickly white color from the blood loss, and his eyes were open wide, as was his mouth...as if he were trying to tell Jessica who had done this gross misdeed to him.

Jessica backed against the wall, looking left and right, as she fumbled her radio from her pocket.

"Mark," she said quietly into the device.

"Yes, ma'am," he replied.

"I just found Jeff Breeden on five. His throat has been cut. Can you do a roll call on the radio, please?"

"Are you sure, Jessica? Is it really Jeff?"

"No, Mark, I thought I'd just make it up for a laugh! Of course I'm sure it's Jeff...and I'm up here alone, unless there's another roving grunt up here somewhere. Please do the roll call! We have to find out who did this, and if it was one of us!"

Mark did the roll call. Jessica heard the names being called off one by one. She kept turning her head from left to right, trying to watch both sides at the same time. Her heart kept hammering as she waited for the roll call to complete.

"Jessica."

"Go ahead, Mark."

He paused. "Five people have not responded. I suggest that you get back on the elevator and get back down here now. I'll send out a general message to everyone to come back to the front desk, and we'll organize a search. We'll find whoever it is."

"That's great, Mark. I'm on my way."

Jessica inched her way to the elevator, and pressed the "down" button. The doors opened immediately, and Jessica stepped in, flipping her hair to the right as she entered. As she did, she heard a silenced shot and felt the whiz of a bullet as it passed close to her ear. The bullet embedded itself in the back wall of the elevator.

Jessica ducked inside the elevator, using the button side to shield her from more gunfire. She took a deep breath, squatted, then fired a shot as she reached around the corner of the elevator door.

No one was there.

Quick glances all around the area she could see from her position confirmed it...whoever had fired the shot had totally disappeared. She remained alert, weapon aimed at out the elevator door, as the doors slid shut.

Oh, my God! That was close! If I hadn't flipped my hair out of my eyes when I did, I'd be dead right now!

Jessica realized that she had been crying for the last minute or so. She reached up and punched the button for the lobby.

There's a killer in the building...and this killer has skills!

"SO, IF THE DOOR IS guarded with computer controlled automatic weapons, how can we get the C-4 up there?" Misty asked.

Louie stared at the door, thinking...well, he stared more at the dead cop than the door. *How the* hell *did I miss somethin' like that?*

"Louie," said Misty.

Louie didn't hear her.

"*Louie!*" she said forcefully, punching his arm at the same time.

Louie jumped. "What the hell, girl? You tryin' to scare the beejeezus outta me?"

"No, I'm trying to get some ideas for getting *this* explosive," she held up a block of C-4, "to *that* door," she pointed to the club entrance, "without getting somebody killed!"

"I'm sorry, Misty," replied Louie. "I'm feelin' bad for my judgement on that cop. I should have checked out the door myself, and figured out what Fernandez had done with it. I got him killed."

"I feel bad that the cop is dead, Louie, but he did it himself. He ran up to the door without any directions from you. If he had been cautious, it never would have happened."

"Maybe."

Misty sighed. "There's a lot that's happened tonight that I wish hadn't, old friend. Right now, I could use some advice on how to get this up there safely."

Louie stared at the grey, putty-like explosive, thinking hard. Suddenly, he snapped his fingers. "I *got* it!" he said, and ran to one of the company's vans.

"*SENOR* Pruett, please pick up the phone," said Fernandez over the club's sound system. "I must speak to you privately."

Pruett picked up the cell phone.

"Those *bastardos* are jamming my camera signals. I can no longer see what is happening."

"What would you like me to do, sir?" asked Pruett.

"It is time to kill someone. Pick one. I don't care who. But they must die slowly and painfully. Use your blade, *senor.* And put me back on the sound system."

"Yes, sir."

Pruett placed the phone in its specially designed cradle, then whispered to one of the men closest to him. The man nodded and stepped down into the pit. At the pit, he chose a woman that looked to be in her mid-thirties, with mousy brown hair, chubby cheeks, and close-set eyes. He shouted at her in Spanish, but she didn't understand. When he poked her hard with the barrel of his weapon and gestured to the catwalk, the woman staggered, as if all of the strength had gone out of her legs. She began a high-pitched keening that started low, but grew louder the closer she got to Pruett.

"*Senors y senoritas,*" said Fernandez through the sound system. "It is again time to try to persuade Joey Justice to surrender. *Senorita, como se llama?* What is your name?"

The woman continued to wail.

"*Shut* UP!" screamed Pruett into the woman's face.

Startled, the woman stared into Pruett's face. "Dawn."

"Dawn," said Fernandez. "Do you have another name that you wish to share?"

"No."

"Are you sure?"

"Yes."

"Justice. Surrender to me now, and I will spare this 'Dawn'...remain where you are, and she will die screaming. Which do you choose?"

The woman's eyes had widened, and she began to struggle against the men holding her, but her resistance was a waste of time. Panic crept into her face as she moved her head from side to side. She began keening again.

"Very well, Justice. Her death is in your hands. Pruett, I want that noise she's making to stop. I want to hear screams of pain. Do you understand, *senor?*"

With a smirk, Pruett said, "Yes, sir." Pruett reached out delicately with the point of his knife and flicked an inch-wide cut on one of the woman's chubby cheeks.

Realization came to the woman's face that her fate was to be cut to ribbons, just seconds before the pain hit. She screamed, loudly and with vigor. The men holding and surrounding her ripped her clothes from her, as Pruett began methodically making small, one to two inch cuts on her body. Some were deep, and some were merely scratches. With one almost hysterical giggle, Pruett sliced off one of the woman's nipples.

It became unspeakable.

AFTER THE WOMAN'S EIGHTH scream, Joey could stand no more. Whispering between clenched teeth, he picked up his radio.

"J-1 to J-2," he said, with eyes tightly shut.

After a second, Misty answered. "J-1, why are you breaking silence?"

He took a couple of deep breaths. "I can't keep listening to these poor people being tortured, J-2. It's unbearable." He shut his eyes tightly and brought the radio down to his knee for a moment, then brought it up again. "I'm going to give myself up."

Misty's response was immediate. "You will *not*, J-1. Repeat: you will not surrender! These people are giving us the time we need to get you out of there, and you will *not* let their deaths be for nothing, *do you understand?*"

Tears rolling down his face as Dawn's screams became hoarse and repetitive, he said, "I hear you, J-2. But you have to break through soon, okay? I mean it!"

Through tears of her own, Misty said, "Oh, my love...we're doing what we can! Just hang on. Please."

IN THE ELEVATOR LOBBY, Jessica called, "Mark!"

"Clear!" he responded.

Jessica rounded the corner toward the front desk. Mark Haase stood, gun in hand, watching the first floor as much as possible, covering Jessica's approach.

Safely behind the desk, she asked, "Is everyone on the way?"

"They are. And I urged extreme caution."

"One thing: tell them that whoever it is has skills. They should watch their backs as well as their fronts."

"How did you find that out?"

"They took a shot at me. I turned, and they had disappeared. It was fast. Very fast."

Mark picked up his cell and sent a group text to all who had responded to the roll call.

"How do we want to break down the search?"

"Let's wait until everyone is here. Mark, this worries me. How did somebody get in here without us knowing it?"

Mark shook his head, not wanting to say the obvious. "Could it be an employee?"

"I didn't want to say it, either, Mark," she replied. "But the thought *did* cross my mind."

"*ohmygodohmygodohmygodohmygodigottagetouttahereicannotstandthisitstoomucht*" whispered Miriam continuously.

Steve went to calm her, while Patty and Tony moved to stand shoulder to shoulder, blocking the sight of them. Brandon stood several feet away from them, watching the guards. The three Justice Security co-workers stood ready to start shooting the guards if it became necessary to protect Miriam and Steve. After all, the two news hounds were under their protection.

The gruesome execution on the catwalk was over. Pruett had breathed heavily as the woman had died. The woman had finally gone catatonic, and could not be returned to consciousness. Finally, Pruett had slit her throat and watched her lifeblood gush steadily from the wound, until she died.

Patty had to look away, as did Brandon. Tony kept his face forward, but was only able to do it by watching the guards across the pit and not looking at the catwalk.

Tony was thinking. *How the hell are we going to get out of this? The kids and I are outnumbered seven to one, even with the boss helping. Even if we take out all of the guards, we still have to get out of this steel ball, and if what I've heard about Fernandez is right, the place is bound to be booby-trapped somehow. I'm getting too old for this shit, I really am.*

Patty moved her hand toward her ear. Tony knew that she was listening to her radio. She casually walked over to Tony, and spoke into the transmitter.

"J-2, this is P-1. I'm with the Captain, can you please repeat?"

"I said, get ready for some fireworks. We have fireworks prepared for the front. Keep your fingers crossed, guys!"

Tony looked at Patty. "Go tell Brandon to be ready for anything, and I'll warn our reporter friends. Misty's getting ready to blow some C-4 on the front door. Let's hope it works."

JOEY HAD BEEN STRETCHING the stiffness out of his legs when Misty's announcement came across the radio. He gathered his meager weapons and prepared as best he could...if only it would work!

LOUIE HAD TAKEN A SMALL magnetic calendar off of the wall of one of the company's vans.

"Let me have the C-4," he said to Misty.

Louie began pressing and stretching the explosive until it was the same size as the 5x7 calendar. He laid the calendar face down on top of the explosive. Both calendar and explosive were no more than an inch and a half thick. He opened a tool box from the back of the van and pulled out a roll of thin, lightweight, aluminum-alloy tape.

He said to Misty, "This is metal duct tape. It's used to patch small holes in shipping containers well enough to keep moisture out. It should hold the calendar to the explosive."

Dexter and Megan had come up to the van while Louie was preparing the C-4.

"What's the use of the calendar?" asked Misty.

Megan smiled, as did Dexter.

"May I, Louie?" asked Megan.

Louie smiled. "Be my guest, honey."

Megan took the package and backed away from the van. At a distance of five feet, she took the package and tossed it toward the van door, with the back of the calendar facing the van. The explosive package hit the side of the van and stuck there.

Misty was amazed.

"See, the magnetic backing on the calendar is just strong enough to support the weight of the explosive, and we don't have to get close to apply it," said Louie.

Megan took the package back to the van, and inserted a wireless receiver into the putty-like explosive. She picked up the wireless controller to the detonator, and turned back around.

"Ready?" she asked Misty.

Misty nodded as she spoke. "Yes, but let's find Marcus and tell him what's about to happen."

When they found Marcus and explained what they were about to try, he was enthusiastic.

"Guys, I don't care if you blow the place to smithereens, as long as it gets those people out," he said.

"So, who's going to get close to the door and throw the explosive at it?" asked Megan.

Everyone looked at Misty. She took a deep breath.

"Dexter, you're the fastest of us," she said. "Would you?"

"Sure!"

Dexter took the explosive and walked until he was about five feet from the entry door. He judged that this was a safe distance, based on what Louie had said about the weapons guarding the door, and tossed the explosive brick to the door. It hit the door and stayed there, held in place by the calendar magnet. He went back and took cover with everyone else.

Megan entered the final code into her wireless controller, and looked at Misty.

"Ready?" Megan asked.

Misty looked around. Everyone was safely away from the front door of the club. She looked at Dexter, who shrugged. She looked at Louie. He nodded. She looked at Marcus. He nodded.

"Let's do it," said Misty quietly, and then held her breath.

Megan pushed the button, and the C-4 exploded with a fairly loud "*WHUMPF*". Smoke billowed from the entry door, blocking it from view. As the smoke cleared, it became obvious that, while charred black in places and dented slightly from the blast, the door remained in place.

"*SHIT!*" shouted Misty, stamping her foot.

"Aw, *man!*" said Louie in disgust.

Megan looked confused. "Maybe a bigger block of explosive would pierce that armor. What do you think, Dex?"

Dexter shook his head as he said, "I don't know, my love. That was a pretty big charge."

Misty had frozen, her thoughts in high gear.

Marcus said, "Misty, would you like to try another charge?"

"Megan," said Misty slowly. "What did you just say?"

"I asked Dexter what he thought."

"No, before that."

Thinking, Megan replied, "I said that maybe a bigger block of explosive would pierce that armor."

Misty's eyes lit up. "Megan, you're a genius! Here's what we're going to do...Go to the van, and, if you brought everything I asked for, we'll need..."

Chapter 9

Inside the club, Joey had waited patiently for his chance to come out from his hiding place and extract a little vengeance of his own. When the explosion came, it was fairly loud inside the club. He waited to hear from Patty, Brandon, or Tony that the nut had been cracked.

But, the word, when it came, was that the club had not been cracked open. Patty was apologetic.

"I'm so sorry, J-1," she said.

Fernandez, however, took the news almost with glee.

"So you see, *senors y senoritas,* my fortress cannot be shattered by mere explosives!" he bragged through the sound system. "You will not be leaving until Esteban Fernandez says you are leaving!"

Joey was beginning to believe him.

"OKAY, TWO GROUPS OF three will conduct the search. Three people will remain here at the desk. The remaining four people will pair off and guard the doors and elevators, staying within sight of each other and of the front desk. Any questions?" said Jessica.

She looked over her group of people. Two more were unaccounted for, but had answered the roll call. That scared her. Of the twenty in the building, they were down to thirteen. Seven either dead or missing.

Of the thirteen left, there were three cafeteria workers and two janitorial people. That left Jessica, Mark, and six grunts to search the entire building for a killer...or killers. All of them were armed, and knew some martial arts skills. The amount of martial arts varied from person to person, but all were good with handguns.

"A couple of things," she continued. "We don't know who we're looking for, and we don't know how many. With so few of us, we are going to have to look out for each other, and make sure that we're all covered. We can't afford to lose another person. Clear?"

Nods from the people.

"Okay, Mark. You will remain here at the desk to field calls or anything else that may pop up. You," she pointed to one of the janitorial staff, then the other, "and you, stay here and guard Mark. You three," she pointed to the cafeteria workers, "watch the stairwell doors and the elevator area. I'll take Teresa Jarrell and Mike Rychen, and Susan Reeves will take Sammy Moore and Don Commisky. Now, that leaves Susie White," Jessica said, pointing to the last uniformed grunt. "Susie, I want you to rove around the lobby here. Make sure that no one gets hurt, or misses an intruder." Susie nodded. "Okay, let's go, people! My group will take the sixth floor, and Susan's group will take the fifth floor. Please ignore the dust on my furniture as you enter my apartment."

People spread out, heading for their assigned search areas. In the elevator area, Jessica pressed the "up" button. Elevator doors slid open immediately, and the six people climbed aboard. Someone pressed the buttons for 5 and 6, and the doors slid shut.

"Be ready for anything, people. Teresa, Mike...be ready to give these guys cover as they dismount the elevator," said Jessica.

Jessica, Teresa, and Mike readied their weapons, as did Susan, Sammy, and Don. At the fifth floor, the doors slid open, showing six people aiming their weapons out at the hallway. Nothing moved.

"Okay, out you go," said Jessica. Susan, Sammy, and Don all exited the elevator and prepared to search the floor. The doors slid shut, and the elevator climbed to the sixth floor. Again, the doors slid open, revealing nothing in sight. Jessica and her two grunts eased off of the elevator.

Both hallways were clear, from the elevator to the sides of the building. All of the apartment doors within sight were closed. The sixth floor of the Justice Security building contained residential apartments for the company's partners, although Jessica chose a smaller apartment on the fifth floor for her home. As the group exited the elevator, Teresa and Mike immediately turned to their left, weapons ready. Nothing in sight.

The closest apartment was a few feet into the long hall, and the first door on the right.

"Joey and Misty's apartment," said Jessica. While the others watched the hall, Jessica tried the knob. The door was locked. She dug out her passkey, and opened the door. She tapped Mike on the shoulder to indicate that he was to enter the apartment with her. They swung into the apartment, scanning the living room thoroughly.

"Okay, Teresa," said Jessica. "Come in, but close the door behind you."

Teresa entered the apartment, but she backed in, keeping her attention on the hall outside. Once inside the apartment, she closed and locked the apartment door.

"Okay, we stay together. I'll open doors and things that look big enough to hide someone. Mike, you cover me, and be ready to fire. Teresa, your job is to watch all around us, so that we don't get taken by surprise. Any questions?"

There were no questions.

The hall closet to their left was their first stop. Jessica grasped the knob, turned it slowly, then threw the door open. All three people aimed their weapons at...coats, long dresses in plastic, and an upright vacuum cleaner. No people.

All three had been holding their breath, and all three let them out at the same time with one big 'whew'.

"I can just see us explaining to Misty why we shot the hell out of her vacuum cleaner," said Jessica. "I'm glad we showed some restraint."

Teresa and Mike both laughed nervously.

"I can see that this is going to take a while," said Jessica. "Especially if we do it the way we should." She looked at the two grunts. "Ready, guys?"

They nodded.

PRUETT'S MEN CARRIED the body of another hostage from the catwalk to somewhere in back of the club. This one had been a young man. Fernandez' voice came over the sound system again.

"Can no one bring me Joey Justice? Is there one of you...just *one*...that can tell me where he hides? I am disappointed."

Mayor Gould had had enough, and said as much to his group.

"It's time to put a stop to this mayhem," he said indignantly. He stood, and straightened his suit jacket. "Will you come with me, Morris?"

Morris looked at the mayor. "Come with you *where,* you selfish windbag?"

A flash of anger crossed the mayor's face. "Up *there,* Morris! On the *catwalk!* Save a few lives, right?"

The deputy mayor gave the mayor a look of disbelief. McIllwain took Gould's arm and almost pulled it out of its socket. "C'*mere,* you pompous idiot!" Once they were relatively out of everyone's earshot, McIllwain let go of Gould's arm. "I don't particularly like you, Gould, but I don't really want to watch you die, either."

"What the hell are you talking about, McIllwain?"

"I know you're dirty, Gould. You as much as admitted it to that reporter, just before you threatened her life. I know you think that because you took a little money from Fernandez, that it makes you invincible. But, Glenn, *you're wrong!* Something like that, it doesn't make you immune! It makes you a damn target! Fernandez doesn't care who you are, and he won't listen to you just because you were willing to take his money!"

"What the hell do *you* know about it, Morris? You've never taken a dirty dollar in your life! What makes you an expert?"

McIllwain sighed. "Because Fernandez is *insane,* Glenn. It won't matter to him that you're on the payroll. Hell, he'll think he's saving money by killing you! I'm just asking you not to do what you're thinking about doing, okay?"

Gould stood as straight as he could, and pulled his jacket down again. "Objection noted...and rejected, Morris." He waved a hand across the pit. "These people are *voters,* man!" He shook his head. "I have to try."

Gould turned and headed toward the catwalk. It seemed that instead of blocking him, the crowd actually parted to allow him smooth passage through them. Morris watched as he approached the catwalk, too stunned to try to intervene.

Gould, on the other hand, started talking as soon as he got into Pruett's earshot.

"Pruett!" said Gould, waving his hand. "Pruett! I need to speak to you! Now!"

A couple of the guards aimed their weapons at the mayor, but Pruett touched their arms and called them off.

"What do you want, *Mis*-ter *May*-or?" asked Pruett in a mocking, singsong voice.

"For Christ's sake, man, bring me up there! I can't shout it for everyone to hear, can I?"

Pruett studied Gould for a moment, then nodded to the two guards. The men descended to the mayor and escorted him to Pruett's place on the catwalk. The mayor, not watching where he stepped, slipped in some blood on the stage, and almost fell. It took massive concentration on the mayor's part to keep his gorge down.

"Pruett, I need to speak to *Senor* Fernandez."

"I can hear you, *Senor* Mayor," said Fernandez through the club's sound system. "You may speak freely."

"Sir, I'd rather speak quietly," replied Gould. "Just you and I, please."

"But, of course! *Senor* Pruett, if you please..."

"Yes, sir!" said Pruett.

TONY ARMSTRONG EASED over to Steve.

"Think your little camera can pick up the mayor?" he whispered.

Steve nodded, then showed Tony that he was already recording.

"Is it too far to pick up sound?" asked Tony.

Steve shook his head.

Tony nodded his understanding. "Guard that camera with your life, brother. I got a feeling you're gonna get the story of your life."

Steve nodded.

PRUETT HAD HANDED A cell phone to the mayor.

"Now what would you like to talk to me about, *Senor* Gould?" asked Fernandez.

Gould had turned his back to most of the people in the pit, and he spoke quietly and firmly into the phone. "*Senor*, you must stop this killing! There's no way I can cover this up!"

"What makes you think I want you to cover this up?"

Gould was caught by surprise.

"You...but...," he stammered into the phone.

"I am going to do two things tonight, *Senor*. I am going to kill Joey Justice, and *I am going to make your city fear me!*"

"But, Esteban, you can't..."

"*What?* First, you presume to tell me to stop killing, then you tell me that I can't! Let me make one thing *very* clear to you, *Senor*: *You do* not *presume to tell me what I can and cannot do!* Are we both clear on this point, Mayor?"

Gould unconsciously straightened his stance. "Yes, *Senor*."

"One last thing, Mayor: you will *never* presume to call me by my first name again."

"Yes, *Senor*."

"Now, you will hand the phone back to Pruett."

Wordlessly, he handed the phone back to Pruett. Pruett held the phone to his ear.

"Pruett? Are you there?"

"I am, *Senor* Fernandez."

"Kill him. Now."

Pruett connected the special cell phone back to the sound system, and looked at Gould, who had turned toward Pruett. Gould had opened his mouth as if to speak to Pruett when the club manager drew his pistol and shot the mayor between the eyes.

"OKAY, GUYS, LOOKS LIKE all's clear here," said Jessica. They had just finished going through the next apartment on the sixth floor. This one belonged to Dexter and Megan.

"Are you sure they live there, Jessica?" asked Teresa. "There didn't seem to be much there."

Jessica smiled. "That's because Dexter has adopted a large part of an Oriental lifestyle. Simplicity and harmony."

"Everywhere but the bedroom," mumbled Mike, who had noticed the mussed covers on the bed and the clothes on the floor.

"Secure that, Mike. You never would have seen it if we weren't looking for a killer," admonished Jessica.

"Yes, ma'am."

The group turned the corner, preparing to enter Louie's apartment. Jessica was still speaking.

"Remember, we're not entering these private areas for our entertainment, or to discover any 'dirt,'" she said. "We're doing it to ensure the building's security. So, anything you see needs to be kept to..."

Mike Rychen's head snapped back, and Jessica's sentence was never finished. Embedded in the center of his forehead was a throwing star, a five-pointed, razor-sharp, metal star. Only half of the star was visible. The other half was inside Mike's head, and had penetrated his brain. He slowly slid to the floor. Teresa and Jessica immediately retreated back around the corner.

"Holy shit!" shouted Teresa.

"Intruder on six, man down! Repeat, intruder is on the sixth floor, and has killed Mike Rychen!" shouted Jessica into her radio. "Mark, do you copy?"

"Copy that, Jessica!" replied Mark.

"This is team two," said Donald Commisky, on Jessica's radio. "On our way for backup now!"

"*Dammit!*" said Jessica. "This one has *skills!* But, who the hell is it?"

Teresa was sobbing quietly as she looked around, a look of terror on her face. "I don't want to die, Jessica."

"We won't, Teresa," replied Jessica, although she wondered if that was a promise she could keep. She had already blundered by letting her guard down as they rounded the corner to Louie's, and now Mike was dead because of it. She needed to remember that this intruder...or intruders...were almost as good as Dexter, and that all of them needed to keep their attention focused at all times.

Jessica registered a noise that sounded like "schploik" at the same time that she was splattered with warm liquid. She turned to Teresa in time to see the woman collapsing onto the floor. Her face had exploded onto Jessica as the silenced bullet had entered the back of her head. Jessica raised her pistol and fired a shot down the hall toward the spot the bullet had to have come from, and then ducked around the corner quickly. Her mind registered that Louie's door was four feet away, and she had the key. She also registered that if an intruder was in the hall, there was a good chance that no intruder was in Louie's apartment. She sprinted the short distance. In front of the door, she fumbled around in her pocket until she found the keys, then she had a few tense seconds in which she couldn't get the key into the lock. Finally, the key slid home and the door opened. She slammed the door behind her and locked it. As she did, a thrown knife embedded itself in Louie's door, with two inches protruding at an angle into Jessica's side of the door. When the knife 'thunked' into the door, Jessica let a small scream of surprise erupt. She leveled her pistol, aimed directly at the spot with the knife. She was almost hyperventilating.

The knife was no longer in the door.

Jessica couldn't believe it. She had been staring directly at it, and never saw it move, but it was gone.

Jessica grabbed for her radio.

"Team two, team two, intruder has killed Teresa. I am trapped inside Louie's apartment. Use extreme caution entering the sixth floor," she said into the transmitter. "Mark, did you copy that?"

"I did, Jessica," he replied quietly. "What are your instructions?"

"Simple. Stay alive."

"THIS WON'T WORK."

"Sure it will."

"Misty, I'm telling you: if the C-4 didn't work, this won't work," said Louie.

"I think you're wrong, big man," said Megan.

"We can at least try it," said Dexter.

"Can I register a concern?" asked Marcus. "Firing a bazooka in the city limits is usually frowned on."

"It isn't a bazooka, Marcus," said Misty. "It's a rocket launcher. Dexter used it on Fernandez before."

"Yeah, but it didn't work then, remember?" said Dexter.

"And it ain't gonna work now!" said Louie. "Whatever that armor is made out of isn't even gonna blush from that thing, much less open it up!"

"What if that thing blows up before it flies away?" asked Marcus.

Misty shook her head. "It *won't*. Jeez, guys, let me at least try it!"

The other four people looked at each other. Dexter shrugged, then said, "Go ahead, Misty."

"Before you do, do you mind if I at least clear the parking lot?" asked Marcus.

Misty sighed. "Sure, Marcus. If it makes you feel better."

BRANDON STOOD NEXT to Tony.

"Boss," he said.

"Um-hm," replied Tony.

"Why don't we just open up on the bad guys right now? I mean, we have machine guns, and chances are really slim that they'd even get a chance to fire at us, much less take us all out."

Tony considered it. *The boy may be right*, he thought to himself. *If we caught them with their guard down just a little bit...*

"Let me think about it for a little, kid," he said to Brandon. "It might be a good idea."

Brandon smiled.

Tony ran the idea over in his mind. *It just might be what we need...then the boss could come out of his hiding place, and...*

"OKAY, FIRE AWAY," SAID Marcus. "Everyone is on the back side of the club...except for us, of course."

"Thanks, Marcus," said Misty. She lifted the rocket launcher to her shoulder and aimed. "Get ready, everybody! Fire in the hole!"

Misty pulled the trigger. The rocket flew to the club entrance, hit it, and ricocheted into the parking lot, burying itself in the Justice Security van's right rear tire. It exploded, and set off the remaining C-4, becoming an even bigger explosion. What remained of the van burned merrily until firemen rushed around from the back of the club, and began spraying water at the flames.

"I don't fuckin' believe it," said Louie quietly. "You as bad as Joey, blowin' up shit by accident!" His eyes left the van and focused on Misty. He pointed at the fire and said, "That's our fuckin' *van*, girl! And you blew it *up*!"

Dexter started shaking his head as he looked at the ground. Megan started laughing.

"You seein' this shit, Dex? She blew it right the fuck *up!*"

Only Marcus noticed the tear as it left Misty's eye.

"Sheeyitt. It's like Joey's doin' it by remote control or somethin'." Louie turned to Misty again. "I know it's fun, blowin' things up, but you gotta..." He stopped because he, too, noticed the tear. "Aww, shit, Misty, I'm sorry, girl."

Megan and Dexter had turned and noticed the tear.

Misty lowered the rocket launcher and wiped at her eye with the back of her hand.

"I'm sorry, guys," she said. "You don't understand. All I want is to get my man out of there safely." She looked up at the group. "He proposed to me." She wiped her other eye. "Finally, he proposed to me. He loves *me,* and he wants me to be his wife. Not just the girl he lives with...no, he wants me to be his *wife."* She threw the rocket launcher onto the ground in disgust. "And now, because of this insane *asshole,* my man might be taken away any minute, and I don't know if I can handle that. I just want Joey *out,* and I want him in my arms, and I want him out *now!"* She burst into tears. "He...he's all I got. He *loves* me." She crossed her arms over her knees and cried quietly.

Louie and Dexter looked at the ground sheepishly. Marcus knelt beside her and put his arm around her shoulder. Megan knelt in front of her, and put her hands on Misty's arms.

"Honey, we're gonna get him out. We just haven't found the right thing to pierce that armor," said Megan.

Marcus said, "You once told me that you had done covert work for the CIA and other uber-top secret stuff. I know you guys, and I know that you *had* to have saved some stuff from those missions! You told me that a lot of your equipment was better than the stuff that the *Bureau* uses. And you're telling me now that there's *nothing* in the lower levels of that building that can take out this Mexican bastard's armor?"

Louie's eyes suddenly widened. He raised his head and grabbed Dexter's arm.

"Dex!" he said excitedly. "We got that..."

"I *know!*" interrupted Dexter. "That'll do it, all right!"

Marcus looked at them. "What are you talking about?"

Megan suddenly smiled. "I think I know what they're talking about, and it just might be the thing!"

Louie said, "Marcus, can we borrow your car? See, Dex and Megan came with me in the van and..." He gestured toward the flaming vehicle, currently being showered with water.

Marcus smiled and threw his keys to them. "Drive carefully, please. It's a Bureau car."

"JESSICA, DO YOU COPY?"

Jessica sat on the floor of Louie's apartment, back against a sofa that was about four feet away from the door and that faced the living room. She was still splattered with Teresa's blood, and she was creeping toward shock. Her arms were limp by her sides, gun in one hand and radio in the other. Her eyes were staring at the slit where the throwing knife used to be, but they were very far away. Her mind kept turning over all that had happened within the last few minutes.

Ten people. That's all that's left from the twenty that were here. I've messed up and let them all be killed. I still haven't caught the killer. I don't even know who it is. I haven't even caught a glimpse of him. All I've been able to figure out is that he's very, very good...a lot better than me. I really need Dexter, or even Megan, to help me, but I'll be damned if I call them. I'm going to get up and go catch a killer! I need to rest first...just for a minute...

"Jessica!" said the whispered voice urgently. "Do you copy? This is Donald, and team two. We're right outside Louie's door. Do you hear me, Jessica?"

Jessica's eyes suddenly focused, and she moved the radio to her mouth.

"I'm here! Just a minute, I'll unlock the door."

Jessica stood and unlocked the door. One by one, team two tumbled into the apartment. She slammed and locked the door, and whirled on the team.

"Are you okay? Are any of you hurt?" asked Jessica excitedly.

Sam looked at Jessica. "We're fine, Jessica. We saw Teresa and Mike. Are *you* okay?"

Jessica nodded. "I'm fine, why do you ask?"

The three exchanged looks.

Susan said, very quietly, "Have you looked in a mirror?"

Jessica looked at them quizzically until realization hit her. She ran to Louie's bathroom, and flipped on the light.

The mirror reflected an image that belonged in one of her beloved horror movies. The left side of her head was covered with splattered blood and bits of grey matter that could only be portions of Teresa's brain. The cornea of Teresa's eye rested on her left shoulder.

Jessica opened her mouth to scream, but couldn't make a sound. She then abruptly threw up so hard into the porcelain sink that her vomit splashed over the sides.

Chapter 10

"Give me your radio for a few minutes. Gotta clear something with the boss before we go nuts with Brandon's idea," Tony said to Patty.

Wordlessly, and with a slight smile on her face, Patty handed her radio to her supervisor.

"Goin' to the can. Back in a minute," he told her. Tony glanced at Steve and Miriam. "Patty, fill them in, would you? Make sure Miriam can handle what she's gonna have to do."

"Yes, sir."

Tony nodded to Steve, nodded to Brandon, and then went to the bathroom. Once inside, he keyed his radio.

"J-1, this is T-1. Copy? Click if you hear me."

The radio immediately clicked.

"J-1, we are in a position to take all of these goons by surprise. There are five, repeat five, of us, fully armed and in position. With your approval, we are going to wait for my mark and take these bastards out as quickly as we can. The catwalk is between us and approximately three goons. When you hear us open fire, come out of your hiding place and take out those three men. Now, you know I would *not* risk this if there was any other way, but I actually think that we can catch these guys with their pants down. Do we have your approval, sir?"

There were several seconds of silence.

"T-1, this is J-1. Send those bastards to hell at your first and best opportunity. If there's any way possible, that damned Pruett is *mine!*"

"Copy that, sir. Please stand ready. T-1 out."

"OH. MY. GOD," SAID Misty slowly. "Megan, what are they doing? They could be killed!"

"Honey, it's their job," replied Megan. "They have to do something to save lives. If you were in there, you probably would make the same choices."

Marcus said, "I want to know who's helping them. Tony said that there were five of them, and they're armed and in a position to take them by surprise. By my count, with Joey hiding and Crowe dead, that leaves only Tony, Patty, and Brandon. Who's numbers four and five?"

Misty looked puzzled. "Wow! You're right, Marcus!"

"Could it be the mayor?" asked Megan.

Marcus snorted. "You can count on zero help from that one, unless it directly benefits him."

JESSICA HAD TAKEN A quick shower in Louie's bathroom. As she came out, toweling her hair, she steeled herself and asked questions.

"Okay, did you guys see any signs of the intruder?"

"We saw Jeff. We saw where you had been shot at. No signs of an intruder, though," replied Susan.

"How far did you get checking apartments?"

Sammy replied to this one. "We had just finished up when you called us."

"Yeah, it's easy to check empty apartments," added Donald.

"We found some explosives, though," said Susan. "The fuses were electronic, and very simple. We defused them."

Jessica stood for a moment, lost in thought. "Did you see anyone when you came up here?"

"No, ma'am," answered Susan.

"How did you come up here? Stairs or elevator?"

"Stairs. We could hear the elevator as it passed us, though," replied Susan.

"We figured it was on an automatic setting to go to a resting place below somewhere," said Sammy.

Jessica's eyes widened.

"That's *it!*" she said quickly. "The intruder knew you'd use the stairs, so they took the elevator! Come *on!*"

Jessica led the way, throwing open the apartment door and running down the hall to the elevator. The others were close behind her, weapons drawn.

Jessica skidded to a stop in front of the elevator and stared at the floor indicator above the elevator door.

It was stopped at "2".

Maybe nothing. But, if it were me, I'd take the elevator to 2, and the stairs down to the lobby, then I'd take out...Oh, God!

Jessica took her radio and spoke.

"Mark! Intruder may be on the first floor with you! Are you okay?"

A few seconds of silence increased her worry. When she heard a reply, she almost cried out with relief.

"Jessica, this is Mark. Intruder has wounded or killed everyone on this floor. My position is behind the desk, and I'm returning fire, but I can't get a clear shot. I could sure use backup."

"Mark, I'm with team two. We're on our way." She turned to the three grunts as she pressed the elevator button. "Here's what we do, people: When we get to the ground floor, we run as fast as we can to the front desk to help Mark. Then we'll call for backup from the guys at the club."

"Sounds good, ma'am," replied Susan. "Let's go kick some ass!"

"HEY, WHERE'S MARK?" asked Dexter. "I don't see him."

Louie and Dexter had driven along the front of the Justice Security building so that they could check out the lobby. From their position, they couldn't see the few people that were lying on the floor in different spots along the lobby, all of them either dead or wounded.

Louie had been checking out the desk, too, when he caught a quick glimpse of an inch-long piece of the desk flying up. It had been a fast thing, seen out of the corner of his eye, but he said, "Let's park, and head up to the lobby real slow, okay?"

"Sure. I'd rather be safe than sorry," replied Dexter, as he turned into the driveway leading to the underground levels.

THE ELEVATOR STOPPED at the lobby. All four of the people inside braced themselves for the mad dash to the lobby desk.

"Before the doors open, I just wanted to say that I'm very proud of the way you've all distinguished yourselves tonight," said Jessica.

Before the three grunts could reply, the doors opened. Since the doors faced the desk, it was a straight run from the elevator to Mark's position.

Jessica began a long yell, beginning with "aaaaaaaaaaaAAAAAHHHHHHHH" as she began running. Susan, Sammy, and Donald all joined in.

As they ran, a hole appeared in Donald's head and he fell to the floor, followed by Sammy. The shots rang out as Jessica and Susan began a zigzag run, trying to avoid being shot, too. Susan took a bullet in the chest, and fell in front of the desk. Jessica dove over the desk, and a shot grazed her arm, causing her to drop her gun to the floor behind the desk. Mark grabbed her as she dived in and softened her landing as well as he could.

"Mark, where's the intruder?"

"Behind the elevator shaft."

Jessica noticed that Mark had been wounded in both thighs.

Mark saw her looking. "The bullet went all the way through one leg, and into the other. It didn't come out." He looked over her graze. "Looks like you might have a scar to tell your boyfriend about, too."

Jessica started chuckling, then so did Mark. Jessica stopped laughing as an idea crossed her mind.

"*Boyfriend...boyfriend...*Mark, what happened to Louie's girlfriend? Did she leave?"

Mark gave it serious thought, trying to remember the sequence of events.

"Jessica, I'm not really sure."

"You don't think..." *It couldn't be...could it?*

Jessica grabbed Mark's arm with one hand while she held the second one up to Mark in a standard 'stop' gesture.

"Donna?" said Jessica loudly. "Is there some way we can talk about all this?"

There was almost a full minute of silence, with Jessica and Mark exchanging glances.

A quiet voice said, "How did you know?"

"Honestly? A good guess," replied Jessica. "May I stand up, Donna?"

Silence for a few seconds. "Yes."

"Promise not to kill me?"

"For now, yes."

"Good enough," said Jessica. Using Justice Security's specially developed hand signals, she gave Mark some instructions.

Jessica took a deep breath, then stood up, looking toward the elevators.

Donna had taken off her ski mask, and stood about twenty feet away from the reception desk. She held a throwing knife in each hand, and a Glock pistol in a holster on her right hip. There was a wicked-looking hunting knife in a sheath on her left hip. She appeared calm. She was wearing form-fitting sweat pants and a tank top, with a hooded jacket that was unzipped. There were blood splatters across the jacket and the pants. She also wore what appeared to be smooth, tight-fitting latex gloves.

Jessica almost gasped when she saw the blood splatters. Then realization set in: This woman had killed or wounded twenty people, in a short time, and had planted explosives on the fifth floor, presumably to destroy the upper level of the building. Jessica's eyes narrowed at the woman. It was all she could do to contain herself, and keep from trying to shoot Donna.

"So, what do you want to know, Jessica?" said Donna tauntingly. "Why? That's usually the big question."

"That'll do for a start," said Jessica tersely.

Donna took a couple of steps forward, which brought her away from the elevators and stairwells. "I was ordered to," she replied. "Esteban Fernandez wanted this to be a two-pronged attack. His thinking was to eliminate the head – that would be Joey – and kill so many of his workers, along with causing major damage to his building, that Justice Security would no longer exist." She took another step forward, hands casually at her sides. "The idea for the explosives was his. He specified the fifth floor, because it would bring the sixth crashing down...and maybe pancaking the entire building, like the Twin Towers in New York all those years ago." She looked at Jessica, a small pained expression on her face. "Killing these people does not leave me feeling very ladylike...but it definitely is better to have them dead than me."

Mark, following Jessica's orders, was transmitting every word through Justice Security's radio system. Sensitive microphones in the lobby picked up every word spoken, and well-placed cameras recorded everything. The feed from the security system was wired into the radio broadcasting board at the central desk. All Mark had to do was flip a couple of switches, and the audio was being broadcast across town. Every Justice Security employee with a radio was picking up the audio from Central.

Jessica's mind was reeling from Donna's remarks. "Fernandez? But I thought...you met Louie...I don't understand!"

Donna chuckled. "I arranged to meet Louie. When you're a famous model, you can do things like that. I figured that, as the only unattached male still in the primary partnership, he would be the easiest mark. I was right."

"But...Fernandez?"

"I got into a little trouble a few years ago during a photo shoot in Mexico. Some of the crew unwisely chose to shoot a few speedballs, and invited me to join them. I was arrested. Because of my 'classic good looks', some of the women in the jail told me what I could look forward to from both the jailers and later the prison guards. Esteban offered to 'un'arrest me, and told me that if I wanted to thank him properly, I would agree to learn some special skills that would help me perform some 'personal favors' for him from time to time. I was trained by an Oriental martial arts master."

"Was it Master Li Ke?" came a voice from behind her. "Not as good as Master Kim Po, who trained me, but I recognize his work."

Donna froze. There had been no sound behind her to betray the owner of that voice. "Dexter. How nice of you to join us!"

"Not just Dexter, baby," said another voice that she knew all too well. "Why don't you give up? I really don't want to have to shoot you."

"Louie, my love! I really don't think you have it in you...but you will!" As she said the last three words, she whirled around and threw two knives as hard and as fast as she could at the spot she thought Louie was standing. She had been correct, and they were heading directly for her target.

Dexter dove in front of his friend and caught both knives as he passed in front of Louie and continued to the floor. Louie fired two shots. The first shot caught Donna in the shoulder, and would not have been fatal, if it had not turned her so that the second bullet entered through her other arm and passed into her chest. It buried itself in her lung, and Donna collapsed onto the floor.

Jessica climbed over the desk, talking as she climbed. "Mark, call for ambulances and medical assistance! If Doctor Bishop feels like he can break away from the club, then tell him we need him here. Dexter, will you and Louie help me see if anyone is still alive? If they are, they'll be on this floor!"

Dexter moved away to begin checking on people. Jessica moved in the opposite direction.

Louie only stood in place, arms at his sides, gun still in his hand, staring at Donna. After a few moments, he began slowly moving toward her. When he was beside her, he knelt down. A tear formed in the corner of one eye, and moved slowly down his cheek. He didn't see Jessica as she moved to within a few feet of him.

When Louie sniffed, Donna pulled the hunting knife from its sheath and turned to bury it into Louie. Louie, who had trained for years under Dexter's tutelage, let reflexes take over, and turned sideways. Donna buried the knife hilt deep in Louie's left arm instead of burying it in his chest.

Suddenly, Donna's head jerked roughly backward and hit the lobby floor. The sound of the shot echoed loudly in the lobby.

Jessica stood with her gun hand extended toward Donna.

"Bitch," said Jessica. Jessica then went to Louie. "Should I pull it out, big guy?"

Louie, obviously in pain, replied through clenched teeth, "No, Jessie, just leave it. If you pull it out, it'll bleed more. I can wait for Doc Bishop."

Jessica nodded, then sat down gracelessly in the floor. She nudged Donna with her gun. "I wonder why she thought that giving up love and friendship was the best choice?"

Dexter had come up behind them. "Maybe she had seen how Fernandez kills. We all saw it when he sent us Patti Hoehn's head...remember?"

Jessica looked up at Dexter. "Did you find anyone alive?"

Dexter shook his head. "Only you and Mark."

Jessica's eyes teared up, and she let out a sob. She couldn't help it.

Louie put his good arm around Jessica's shoulder. "I know, Jessie. I know."

After a moment, Dexter said, "Guys, one of us still needs to get that thing to open up the club and take it back." He squatted beside the two of them. "Louie's obviously out of the equation, Jess...that leaves me. Or you, if you want to do it. As a matter of fact, I think it *should* be you...I'd like all of the people gathered there to see that our girls can kick ass with the best of them!"

Louie looked at Dexter. "You know, I think you're right, old friend. It should be Jessica. You and me, we can hang out here and wait. Jessica can inform Marcus – he'll keep the police interference in the building to no more than they need."

"What are you guys talking about?"

"Well, Jessie, it involves some creative driving. And some lifting," said Dexter.

"Driving? I can drive anything that has wheels!" replied Jessica.

"Yeah, girl, but what if it has tracks?" asked Louie.

Chapter 11

"**M**-1, do you copy?" said Dexter over the radio

"This is M-1, D-1. I copy. How is everyone? What happened?" replied Misty.

"Explanations later, Misty. Jessie is on her way with what we thought of. It may take her a few minutes to get there. We had to load a few things onto it."

Puzzled, Misty replied, "Copy that, Dexter. E.T.A.?"

"About ten minutes," came the response. "Has anyone asked Doctor Bishop to come back to the building?"

"He's on his way, Dex...Marcus has people coming to deal with what happened there. He's claimed Federal jurisdiction."

"I copy, Misty. It's up to you girls now. Is Megan around?"

"Right here, handsome hubby."

"Let Jessica take care of the door. She needs the release right now, okay?"

"Dexter, darling, what is she bringing?" asked Megan.

"You'll see, sweet Megan. Hey, I have to go – some Federal suits are at the front door. I love you," said Dexter.

"I love you, too, honey," transmitted Megan.

"*Senor* Pruett, please pick up the phone. I need to speak with you," said Fernandez, through the sound system.

Pruett picked up the phone and said, "Yes, sir?" He began pacing as he talked.

Tony noticed that most of the guards were distracted and seemed bored. They had been standing now for a few hours, and the inactivity was preying on them.

Well, it's now or never, I guess.

Tony walked over to Steve and Miriam. "It's time...Miriam, can you do this?"

Miriam nodded. "Yes. Definitely."

Tony looked at Steve, who nodded slightly. "Good enough. You two get ready," said Tony.

Tony then caught the eye of Patty, who nudged Brandon. Using hand signals, he told them to choose their targets – the time was now. Both turned and aimed their weapons.

Tony moved to their right, basically forming a five-man line along the edge of the pit, each of them aiming for guards along the perimeter.

"*Now!*" shouted Tony.

As the five of them shot at and took out most of the guards, Joey Justice sprang from his hiding place in the pit. He had been hiding inside one of the huge speakers connected to the sound system. When he came through, the back of the speaker collapsed onto the floor. Joey stepped over it, looked up and saw three guards with weapons coming to the ready. Joey, moving toward them, fired a single shot at each of the three, dropping each with a shot to the head. He continued up the stairs to the rim of the pit, just as the remaining guards collapsed and Tony's group ceased firing.

None of the guards remained standing.

Pruett had been shielded from the initial burst of gunfire by two of the guards. He had immediately began running toward his office down the hall from the pit, and he never once looked back. It was time to get out of Dodge!

Joey registered that Pruett was running away, but since the building was still sealed off, Joey wasn't worried about the manager escaping. People had only then began screaming, crying, and generally making noise.

"*Folks! People! LISTEN to me, please!*" shouted Joey. The crowd began to calm a bit, helped along by people in the audience that recognized Joey. "People, we are all safe...for the moment." He pointed across the pit to Tony and his crew. "Thanks to those five people right over there. Three of them work for me: Tony Armstrong, Patty Ferguson, and Brandon King. The other two are Miriam Apple from Channel Seven news, and Steve, her cameraman. Those people took out the guards and relieved the pressure we were facing here. Is the Deputy Mayor here?"

Morris McIllwain stood up. "Right here, Joey!"

"Morris, I would guess that you're the mayor of the city now. Could you let these people know that they're safe right now? I need to go catch the manager of this place!"

McIllwain waved Joey off. "With your people's help, I believe I have it under control! Go!"

Joey yelled to Tony, "Let Misty know that we're okay in here now, and that the main objective is to find a way to get us out of here! I'll be back!"

Joey ran after Ray Pruett with a murderous look on his face.

AFTER HE TALKED TO Misty, Tony walked over to Miriam and Steve. He looked at Miriam until she met his eyes.

"Are you okay?" he asked her.

Slowly, as if making up her mind, she nodded. "I'm fine, Tony." She gestured to the guards. "It was them or me." She looked at Steve, then back at Tony. Slowly, Miriam broke into a smile. "I wanted it to be me. I have a wonderful life...and the biggest goddamn *exclusive* news story you have ever seen in your life! If I don't win the Pulitzer for this one, I never will win it!"

Tony smiled at her, then nodded at Steve. "Good job, ranger."

Steve smiled back.

MEGAN WRAPPED HER ARMS around Misty after Tony signed off, and both women cried in relief.

"Oh, Misty, I *knew* they'd pull it off! Now we just have to get them out of there," said Megan.

"Megan," Misty replied through sobs, "I love him so much! I don't think I could stand it if he got hurt...or killed!"

Marcus was on his cell phone. "Do not stop or hinder Ms. Queen in any way, do you understand? Give her a police escort if you have to – just make sure that she gets here!" He hung up, and chuckled to himself. He turned to Misty and Megan. "Jessica is about two blocks away. She'll be here in a few minutes."

Misty looked puzzled as she wiped her nose with a tissue. "Why are you chuckling about that, Marcus?"

Marcus smiled at his friend. "You'll see, sweetie...you'll see."

PRUETT HAD LOCKED HIMSELF in his office.

Joey had intended to kick it down, but had second thoughts. *If he's in there, there's nothing he can do. We've got him bottled up right now. When I saw that office the first time, I noticed that there were no windows, and only one door. He's not going anywhere!*

Joey pulled out his radio. "Tony, you copy?"

"Yes, sir," came the immediate response.

"If you can spare Patty and Brandon, I'd like them to come guard Pruett's office door. Pruett has locked himself inside, and I want to make sure that he doesn't get out."

"Right away, Joey."

Joey smiled. *Poor Pruett. Once we lock him up, Fernandez will have him killed in jail so that he won't ever have to talk. If I don't kill Pruett first.*

"Joey?" said his radio.

"Go ahead, Misty." He brought the radio up again. "I love you, babe."

Joey could hear the smile in her voice. "I love you, too, Joey. Jessica has just driven to the entrance of the parking lot. I think she brought what we need to get you out of there."

"What did she bring?"

"She brought the tank."

LOUIE HAD TOLD JESSICA that driving the tank was just like driving a Bobcat.

"Ever driven any big machinery?" he asked.

Jessica looked at him. "Oh, every *day*," she replied tartly. "It's my *dream* job, Louie!" Then realization of the people she had lost hit her briefly. "Oh, God,

Percival, it may be the job I need...at least I won't let anyone get killed that way," she said through the tears.

Louie shook his head and held her close with his uninjured arm for a couple of minutes until she got herself under control. "Jess," he said. "You don't have to do this. Dex can take the tank, and you can stay here. They'll want to talk to you, anyway."

Jessica pushed away from him. "No! I can do this! I *need* to do this!"

Louie nodded. "Okay. Now, I can't climb into that thing and show you, so I'm going to ask Dex to show you what you need to know."

Dex had given her a brief driving rundown, and then had pointed to the AP rounds used in the tank's cannon. She had five.

"They're heavy, Jess," Dexter had told her. "I really doubt you're going to need more than one, but, if you do, there are five more over there." And he pointed to a rack inside the turret that housed the rounds. "They're tremendously heavy, so you'll need help lifting one if you have to use more than one."

Jessica steered the tank out of the underground garage. The entrance barely gave clearance to the tank, with only inches to spare from the top and from the sides. She had one bad moment, when she knocked over one of the swing-down gates that hadn't lifted in time for her, but then she was out. As she popped out of the building, she turned a bit quickly and ran over the passenger side of the FBI car parked outside the building, but Jessica quickly got the hang of driving the huge artillery vehicle.

Louie had gotten the FBI men to provide an escort for the tank, complete with sirens and flashing lights. They stopped for no traffic lights, and many drivers stopped their frustrated shouting, honking, and fist-waving when they saw why traffic had been stopped.

Jessica stopped in the middle of the club's entrance, opened the access door on the tank, and popped her head out, waving her hand.

"Misty! Megan! Over here!"

Jessica saw Misty speak into the radio and start walking over to the tank. Megan grabbed Marcus, and the three stopped beside one of the big tracks.

"Nice guns," said Marcus, with rolling eyes.

"Oh, shut up, Marcus, and help them up here!" replied Jessica.

Marcus boosted Megan up first, then Misty. Once they were aboard, Marcus climbed up and in.

"Roomy," he commented.

Jessica pulled Misty over to the controls. "Look, Misty, I know Dexter thinks I should be the one that opens that place up, but I think it needs to be you."

"Me? Why?"

Jessica shook her head. "Something else that Dexter told me: that Joey had finally asked you to marry him."

"He did, but what does that have to do with getting him out of the club?"

"Then you need to show him that you aren't afraid to do whatever it takes to be with him...also, it's great for arguments. You can always say, 'Remember when I saved your sorry butt when Fernandez had you inside that club?'"

Marcus snickered. "I *knew* you women planned things like this!"

Megan giggled at Marcus' remark. "I hope you'll keep it a secret, Marcus."

"Who would believe me?"

"J-1, do you copy?"

Joey grabbed his radio and answered. "I copy, Misty."

"Will you please move everyone away from the entry area? And away from a direct path from the entrance?"

"Sure, give us a few minutes. You copy that, Tony?"

"Sure do, boss. Most everyone is well away, and off to the sides."

"Do what you need to do, Misty."

"Copy, Joey."

MISTY HAD MANEUVERED the tank so that it was directly across from the entrance, and about twenty feet away. She had swung the turret around so that the big gun was aimed directly at the front entrance.

Misty looked around the turret at her companions, then took a deep breath. "I hope this works...Fire in the hole!" She pushed the big button that served as the firing mechanism, and the big gun fired the round. Misty had not counted on how loud the sound would be inside the tank, and neither had the other three. All had seriously ringing ears after the shot went off.

The round, a standard AP, or Armor-Piercing, round, hit the metal door of the club, pierced it, and went through it, angling down the entire way. It imbedded itself just inside the club's entrance, then detonated. With the hole in the door, the entry structure was already compromised, so the explosion of the round blew the door to pieces. It also bent the door frame so badly that the guns spread around the door facing could not extend from their hiding places.

The club was open.

"Tony!" said Joey into the radio. "Take Patty and get these people out of here as orderly as you can! If Miriam is up to it, ask her if she wants to see Pruett dragged out of his office."

There were a few seconds of silence, then Miriam spoke over the radio. "You bet your ass we want to see it! So does Steve, and we'd like to film it if you don't mind."

"I expected you would, Miriam. I'll be waiting on the other side of the pit for you two."

MISTY COULDN'T GET out of the tank fast enough. She climbed down as quickly as she could and ran to the entrance of the club. She stopped long enough to carefully step over the remains of the unfortunate policeman, and, once inside, worked her way around the hole in the floor.

"Joey!" she called as loudly as she could. "Joey! Where are you?"

She ran up the small stairs leading to the pit, then stopped abruptly as she caught a glimpse of what was on the catwalk. It was as if she had just walked into an abattoir, and it was all she could do to keep from vomiting. It was later determined that fourteen people, including their own Jim Crowe, had been killed by Ray Pruett, as ordered by Esteban Fernandez. Dead bodies did not turn Misty's stomach – after all, they had seen much worse in some of their overseas cases – but the mindless, extreme violence of the executions caused her insides to turn flipflops.

Oh, my God! she thought to herself. *All this just to get to Joey? And* me? *How can we ever justify to ourselves the cost of tonight?* She crossed her arms over her stomach.

Tony had spotted Misty as she stood just inside the entrance to the pit room. When she crossed her arms over her stomach, he went to her.

"Boss?" he said.

"Tony," she whispered. "All these people? Killed because of *us?*"

"No, *ma'am,*" Tony said sternly. "Almost every *one* of those people *knew* where Joey was hiding! They *knowingly* went to their deaths to keep him alive, so that he could pay retribution for what happened here tonight, and to show Fernandez that he doesn't own the population of this city! So, yeah, shed a tear for them...they deserve that. They *don't* deserve your pity...or your guilt. Both of those things cheapen their sacrifices! For once, boss lady, I'm telling *you*...don't feel that it was wasted on you or him. It was the ultimate vote of confidence in the two of you, and in Justice Security, to keep Fernandez at bay."

Misty wiped her eyes and sniffed loudly. "You really think so?"

A voice from behind her said, "There's no 'think' to it, Ms. Wilhite. With the exception of my predecessor, each of these people gladly went to their deaths for him...and you. Please don't stop protecting us."

Misty had whirled to see Morris McIllwain, acting Mayor of the city.

"Y-yes, sir," she said quietly.

McIllwain smiled. "Thank you. Now, your man is down that hall on the other side of the pit. I think he'd like to see you right now."

Misty smiled, then leaned up to peck the mayor on the cheek. She looked as if she wanted to say more, but she turned and ran toward Joey.

"*Pruett!*" shouted Joey into the manager's door. "*Come on out! I want to talk to you!*"

Joey was standing outside the door to the fugitive manager's office. Beside him stood Brandon King, Miriam Apple, and Steve the cameraman. All carried Uzis that they had liberated from the guards. Steve was filming.

No response came from inside the office.

"I don't think he can hear you, Joey," said Miriam. "Our private room was soundproofed so much that we couldn't even feel the thrumming of the bass."

Joey nodded. "You're probably right. But I have to try, just in case he *can* hear me."

"JOEY!"

All four of the people outside the manager's office turned quickly toward the shout, just in time to see a flying brunette bombshell in a disheveled evening gown tackle Joey and slam him into the wall with the impact. Three of the people smiled as they realized that the flying bombshell was Misty. The fourth person did not smile...Joey was busy returning a very passionate kiss.

When the kiss ended, Misty said, "Joey, I didn't think I'd get to see you again. I love you, Joey Justice, with all my heart."

Joey pressed Misty's ear against his chest. "Hear that?"

She nodded.

"You put the boom-boom into my heart, Misty. I don't want to go solo through this life." He tilted her head up so that he could look into her eyes. "It's time to scream it from the rooftops, my love." He looked at Steve. "Steve, would you please raise that camera? I have something to say that I hope you folks will broadcast it for me."

Steve looked at Miriam. She smiled at Steve and nodded. Steve raised the camera and gave Joey a "thumbs up" sign.

"My name is Joey Justice. The lady standing next to me is Misty Wilhite. I've been in love with her since college, but I never thought I was good enough to be her husband. Apparently, she believes otherwise, because I asked her to marry me, and she said that she would." He paused for a moment. "Esteban Fernandez has been a burden on Justice Security for quite some time, mainly because he hates me and wants Misty for...well, use your imagination. Tonight, he's killed...or, rather, *had* killed...several innocent people at this night club, and several people at Justice Security that were only doing their jobs." His brows furrowed, and his stare into the camera became intense. "It ends tonight. If you are watching, Fernandez, we're through waiting for you to come to us. You opened the ball, now you're going to see just how much hell you've brought onto yourself. From this point on, Justice Security is after *you*. We're going to cost you money, people, and, eventually, your life – that will be either prison or your death. And you will *never* lay your filthy, blood-covered dickbeaters on this wonderful woman...be it now or after we're married. We're going to get you, Fernandez. Count on it."

Joey looked at Steve, then at Miriam. "Thank you. That's all I wanted to say."

Miriam leaned in to kiss Joey's cheek. "Thank *you*, Joey. Without you and your people, Steve and I wouldn't be alive right now."

Joey blushed, then looked at Brandon and Misty. "Why don't we open this damned door, people? Then we'll bring that bastard kicking and screaming into the light!"

Brandon smiled. "Yes, *sir!*"

The three Justice Security personnel lined up. On Joey's count, they kicked the door in when Joey hit three. They burst in, guns at the ready.

The manager's office was empty. Pruett was gone.

Joey swore so strongly that it would have made a twenty-year Navy veteran blush.

When he took a breath, Misty asked him, "How did he get out, Joey?"

"I don't know, Misty. He had to have a rabbit hole, but where?"

"He's right, ma'am," said Brandon. "He didn't come through the door, and there aren't any windows. There's isn't anywhere to hide in here. Fernandez wanted you two brought to him, and he knew that the entrances would be watched by our people or official personnel, so Pruett *had* to have a rabbit hole...and we'll find it."

The office was sparsely furnished. There was a big desk in front of a set of built-in bookcases, a sectional sofa that wrapped around one corner of the room, a filing cabinet, and a door that led to a bathroom with a shower. Good quality paintings were hung on the soundproofed walls, ranging from small to very large.

The surface of the desk seemed the most likely place to conceal a trigger or button that would open the entrance to a passageway, but Joey and Misty looked over and picked up everything that was there. They then looked along and under the edges. They removed the drawers and searched inside the spaces. They lifted the desk and moved it several feet away. No trigger.

Steve and Miriam stood in the doorway as Steve filmed the search.

Brandon searched the bathroom. He found nothing.

Joey stood with his hands on his hips. "Okay, that leaves the bookcases and behind the sofa. I'll take the bookcases. Misty, would you help Brandon move the sofa?"

Joey was giving the bookcase an eyes-only look-over as Brandon and Misty each grabbed an end of the sofa, intending to slide it out.

The sofa wouldn't budge.

Joey went to the middle and grabbed the middle. He pulled when Misty and Brandon pulled, but nothing happened. The sofa still wouldn't move.

"Okay, let's look under it. Maybe it's screwed to the floor," said Joey.

They looked under the sofa, but it was built so low to the floor that they couldn't see anything.

"Pull the cushions," said Misty.

She and Brandon started taking the cushions off from the ends, while Joey grabbed the middle cushion. Instead of coming off of the sofa, the cushion flipped up. Underneath was a round metal door.

"Found it," said Joey, nodding to himself.

The metal door, or hatch, was a simple design. A flat wheel on top of the hatch spun, then unlatched.

"Stand back. We don't know if this is a trap," said Joey.

Misty and Brandon each moved back a step and held their guns ready, aimed at the hatch. Joey put his hand on the flat metal and turned it until the catch released.

The hatch had a pneumatic system. It popped up, and then open.

Nothing came from beneath.

Joey eased over to the hatch and looked inside.

The hatch had a ladder built into one side, and led down...but they couldn't tell what was at the bottom. Misty had seen a flashlight in the desk, so she retrieved it and gave it to Joey. He used it to illuminate the bottom.

"Hmph. Looks like a sewer pipe," he said. He studied it for a minute, then said, "I'm going down there. Brandon, you stand guard here at the top and be ready to slam this thing shut if anything goes wrong."

"What about me?" asked Misty.

"Babe, please help Brandon, okay? And watch out for Steve and Miriam...don't let them get hurt."

Misty nodded.

Joey slung the shoulder strap of the Uzi over his arm so that the weapon was across his back. He climbed up onto the sofa, then stepped over onto the ladder. He began climbing down.

At the last rung of the ladder, he used the flashlight and looked down. The bottom of the sewer pipe below looked to be about five feet below the ladder.

Pulling his Uzi around under one arm, he held to the ladder and the flashlight with one hand. With a tiny leap backward so that he cleared the ladder, he dropped down into the sewer. Once he hit bottom, he quickly swung his light and weapon left, then right. No sign of Pruett.

Joey took a moment to call back up the escape route. "Looks all clear." He held up his radio. "J-1 to M-2, do you copy?"

"Hi, Joey. What's up?"

"Megan, is Marcus close to you?"

"Ummm...yes, I see him. Want me to get him for you?"

"Yeah, would you please ask him if he'll meet me in the manager's office? Tell him he'll be coming down the rabbit hole."

After a few seconds, Megan came back on the radio. "You really want me to tell him that?"

Joey smiled. "Yep, and tell him to bring a gun...we're going hunting."

DR. CALEB MITCHELL, the one of the two Justice Security staff medical personnel, were busy tending to the wounded...both the physical and the mental. Dr. Mitchell mended, stitched, and put patients on the path to physical healing...then told people to call him at his Justice Security office, and that he would be glad to help them through the emotional trauma at no charge to them. Jessica was assisting Dr. Mitchell as much as she could, and so did various EMT personnel.

Caleb was set up beside the army of ambulances. Marcus was in a small group of people beside the ambulances that included the chief of police, a few FBI suits, a few policemen, and the new Mayor.

As Megan approached the group to retrieve Marcus, she could overhear the Mayor talking.

"...as dirty as the day is long. If he hadn't been executed by Pruett and Fernandez, he would easily have spent the rest of his life in jail." He moved to within inches of the chief of police. "Now, I *know* you're an honest man, Chief, and I know that you don't like Joey Justice or his people. I don't know why, and I don't care why. But I do know this: For all of the violence done tonight, it was Fernandez that made the first move...probably with Gould's blessing. And just because Misty Wilhite injured your ego by telling you to 'shut your cock-holster' doesn't mean that they're guilty of anything besides self-defense, or the defense of others in mortal danger. If *any* of these fine people are even ticketed for jaywalking by any of your police force, you will find yourself walking a street beat in Hooker Hollow, or out of a job completely. Am I clear on this subject?"

Marcus and the other FBI men were all hiding their smiles behind their hands or looking in other directions. Megan had to hide a smile as she came to Marcus and relayed Joey's message. Marcus nodded, then turned toward the group.

"Please excuse me, Mayor McIllwain," he said. "I have to join Joey for something, but I would like to say this to the Chief: Sir, this entire evening, both here and at the Justice Security building, is under Federal jurisdiction, and any Justice Security personnel may be viewed as Federal agents performing their duty. I expect you to treat them as such. Thank you, gentlemen."

Megan was snickering to herself as she walked with Marcus into the club. Marcus did a really good job keeping his snickering to himself.

"CALEB?"

"Yes, Jessica?"

"Am I a jinx?"

"Not at all, Jessica. Sit down, and let's talk about it."

JOEY SMILED AS MARCUS joined him in the sewer.

"Okay, I'm here," said Marcus. "And I've probably ruined a great pair of shoes."

"I'll buy you a new pair of shoes," replied Joey. "This is where Pruett disappeared. Which way do you think he went?"

Marcus took the flashlight and looked in one direction for a few minutes, then he looked in another.

"Want the truth?" asked Marcus.

Joey nodded.

"He's gone, Joey. Give it up."

Joey looked down at the trickle of sewer water for a moment.

"Yeah, that's what I thought. *Shit!*"

Chapter 12

In the remote town of Playa Boca Chica on the western coast of Mexico, just west of the Sierra Madre mountains and south of the city of Colima, there is a beautiful 27-room *hacienda*. It is approximately half a mile from the Pacific beach, and is located just outside the city limits.

The estate is five acres, and is surrounded by a solid stone fence, ten feet high. Armed Federal soldiers patrol the fence, both inside and outside. Alarms are installed everywhere, and the driveway gate is remotely operated. Attack dogs are kept in cages around the estate, ready to be unleashed at a moment's notice. Security of the estate is paramount.

After all, this is the home of a general in the Mexican army.

It is the home of General Esteban Fernandez.

NINETEEN SEPARATE FUNERALS were held for the employees of Justice Security killed in the line of duty the night of the attack. Almost every employee not on duty attended each funeral.

At the funeral of Jim Crowe, Tony Armstrong asked, and received permission, to deliver a eulogy. It was filled with high praise, and told of Jim Crowe's stalwart bravery in the face of unavoidable death. There wasn't a dry eye in the house.

The company memorial services for the nineteen people were combined into one. Each name was solemnly placed on the memorial wall in the lobby that contained names of other brave personnel that gave their lives in the line of duty. Crowe's name plaque was placed beside the shadow box containing Gus Brazzle's name and keepsake stuffed "sugar" bear, a grim reminder that, sometimes, there *are* things worth dying for.

The owner of Justice Security's rival company, Jim Dandy, attended the memorial service as a professional courtesy. He had told Joey that he felt he needed to, because, but for the grace of God...well, you understand.

THE MASTER BEDROOM at the General's fortress contained an architectural wonder: A *very* well-hidden entrance to a stairwell, accessed by pulling not one, but *three* separate books into a leaning position in a specified order. The bookcase then slid to one side, exposing the stairs. The stairs were carved from stone, and led down thirty feet to a large stone dungeon. The General's home was constructed on the grounds containing the ruins of an old Spanish castle, and the ten-room dungeon was all that remained. It was forgotten by the entire town.

Since the General's arrival, many people died screaming within those walls. Very few of the screams had travelled outside of the General's walls, but, occasionally, when the wind was right, they could be heard in Playa Boca Chica.

It is only the wind, thought the locals.

"WELL, JOEY, YOU GOT your wish," said Marcus.

Joey, Marcus, and the other partners were all seated in Joey's office in the couches and soft seats. Marcus was bringing interesting news.

"The U. S. Government will finance your hunt for Fernandez, within a reasonable limit. The financing will not appear in any shape, form, or fashion as coming from the government, and if any of you are caught outside the country, the United States will publicly disavow any knowledge...but, privately, the CIA will be relentless in making certain that you are freed unharmed. In return, you agree to testify in very closed-door, top-secret House and Senate Intelligence committees about what you learn about the drug pipelines into the U. S., and anything you deem necessary to the security of the nation," said Marcus. "I have to formally ask: Is this acceptable to you folks?"

The six partners shared looks around the glass coffee table.

"Finest kind," said Joey. "That means 'yes.'"

"Yeah, and right now, all we're worried about is inside our own borders," said Louie.

Megan nodded. "Louie's right. We've got enough to target right here in the States."

"We can worry about other countries later," said Dexter.

Each partner added his or her signature to the contract Marcus had brought with him.

"AND, SO, THE TRUE HEROES of our city that night were not the firemen, policemen, or even Justice Security. The true heroes of our city were the men and women that gave their lives to protect Joey Justice, and to give him the opportunity he needed to save everyone else," said Miriam Apple, into the camera focused on the Channel 7 news desk.

"As a result of these brave, selfless people, those of us left from inside of that club that night will continue to live...to contribute...and to be responsible for ourselves, our families, our friends, and our neighbors. I consider myself lucky to have helped that night...not by killing people, that is never acceptable if there is another choice. I'm lucky to have been accepted and included in making a plan happen to save others. And we'll all say silent prayers of thanks for blessing this city with Justice Security's brave members. I know I will."

"LOOK, I REALIZE THAT Joey doesn't want any publicity or recognition from the city, but I have to do something," said new Mayor Morris McIllwain into the telephone. "It's a new dawn on a new city!"

RAY PRUETT GRADUALLY became aware that he was waking up.

It began as a need to pee, resulting from the steady drip of water from somewhere behind him.

Only one drop, every few seconds: *drip...drip...drip.*

Almost enough to think of a leaky faucet...or something perpetually damp.

The next thing he realized was that his wrists and arms hurt, and that he couldn't feel his hands.

Pruett tried to see above his head, but the darkness prevented that. He could not, however, bring his hands to his sides.

Where the hell am I? The last thing I remember is...

Esteban Fernandez. And Felix Juarez, right hand man to Fernandez. When Pruett came out at the designated manhole cover, he went inside the Embassy Suites in the ritzy part of the city. He had gone to the room Fernandez had told him to go to, and Juarez had let him into the room. When he walked in, he remembered saying, "I am so sorry, *jefe*," and then everything went black.

Now I'm here...but where is here? And why do I hurt?

Then Pruett became aware that he was only able to touch the floor with his toes.

Oh, God...now what the hell?

In the darkness, he heard a rhythmic squeaking, coming closer.

Pruett almost wanted to scream.

With sudden brightness, a halogen spotlight appeared over his head. Pain stabbed into his eyes as the light broke the darkness. Finally, he was able to see.

Pruett's arms were locked tightly at the wrist by chains and cuffs hanging from the ceiling, beside the spotlight. Eyes wide with fright, he looked back down.

A wheeled cart was resting beside a folding metal chair. Seated in that chair was Esteban Fernandez. His eyes were much like a shark's eyes, pupils as black as the irises surrounding them, and irises abnormally large. Fernandez rarely blinked, which added to the similarity of a shark's blank stare.

Fernandez had a wide grin on his face, almost a rictus. He was dressed in white coveralls.

"*Jefe*," whispered Pruett. He was terrified.

Fernandez nodded. "In the late eighteen hundreds, the Apaches that hid in the Sierra Madres used to torture their prisoners. They wanted to see how big a man they had caught. The longer a prisoner held out against the torture, the bigger a man they had in their possession...which, of course, reflected on them, making them big for catching a big prisoner."

Grin intact, Fernandez reached over to the top shelf on the wheeled cart, which Pruett noticed had several maroon-encrusted tools on it. Fernandez had selected a scalpel.

"One of their favorite tortures involved cutting small, one-inch strips of skin from the prisoner's body. Many men lasted until they had almost been skinned alive."

He leaned forward and looked into Pruett's wide, scared eyes.

"*Senor* Pruett, let us discuss your failure to deliver either of my enemies to me, shall we?"

IT IS ONLY THE WIND, thought the townspeople.

About The Author: T. M. Bilderback is a former radio announcer with a number of story ideas running around inside his head, most based on or inspired by classic songs. The author currently resides in Tennessee, and is writing feverishly in order to banish these stories from his head and into book form before he runs screaming into the street.

Other works by T. M. Bilderback

Nicholas Turner
    If You Could Read My Mind

Justice Security
Mama Told Me Not To Come
Someone Saved My Life Tonight
Jackie Blue
Wake Me Up Before You Go-Go
Saturday In The Park
MacArthur Park
The Little Drummer Boy
The Night Chicago Died
Jim Dandy
Cow Patty
Hell's Bells
Black Dog
Lido Shuffle

Tales Of Sardis County
Don't Come Around Here No More
Junior's Farm
The Devil's In The Details
I'm Your Boogie Man

Colonel Abernathy's Tales
The Lion Sleeps Tonight
Heart Of Glass

Other Stories
The Wreck Of The Edmund Fitzgerald
Gold
Hot Child In The City
Eli's Coming

Other Novels
Empty Eyes

Story Collections
Greatest Hits

www.ingramcontent.com/pod-product-compliance
Lightning Source LLC
Chambersburg PA
CBHW020658180626
46816CB00003B/1341